SHAMAN IN THE CITY

Vikas Trivedi & Smita Agarwal

ISBN 978-93-5559-103-6
Copyright © Vikas Trivedi & Smita Agarwal, 2022

First published in India 2022 by Leadstart Inkstate
A brand of One Point Six Technologies Pvt. Ltd.

123, Building J2, Shram Seva Premises,
Wadala Truck Terminal,
Mumbai 400022, Maharashtra, INDIA
Phone: +91 96999 33000
Email: info@leadstartcorp.com
www.leadstartcorp.com

Disclaimer: This is a work of fiction. All the names, characters, businesses, places, events and incidents in this book are either the product of the author's imagination or used in a fictitious manner. Any resemblance to actual persons, living or dead, or actual events is purely coincidental.

Editor: Mannat Lumba
Cover: Ilayaraja
Layouts: Ashwini Rane

Contents

About the Authors

Vikas Trivedi is from lake city Udaipur in Rajasthan. He pursued and achieved a master's degree in individual streams of English literature, Psychology, and Political Science, and a Ph.D. in Psychology. He now uses his knowledge and education to teach as a professor of psychology and literature.

Vikas used his knowledge of psychology and the laws of attraction to transform his life and overcome problems, both big and small. His belief in the Universe's power and the results he achieved led to a very interesting phase in his life.

The successful duo together had published their second book, '42 Days of Love', which is inspired by the real-life heroics of an Australian deep-sea diver. Their third book, '14/2: The Attack on Pulwama', is a historical fiction based on the real incident.

Ms. Smita Agarwal hails from Kolkata, West Bengal. As a child, her interests always steered away from academic studies and into creative art. She pursued honours in accountancy and after having graduated, she gave in to her passion for creative work. She ventured into the field of interior designing and received a diploma in computer-aided designing.

Smita also is an extremely knowledgeable and successful Pranic healer, an art she has been practicing for over 13 years. The continual study of Pranic healing is what led her into exploring the powers of the mind, and finally meeting Vikas Trivedi, the two of whom together wrote their debut book 'The Hidden Spark', which became a phenomenon. It received acclaim across India and abroad, and was featured in multiple media channels and newspapers.

'Shaman in the City', which is a gripping psychological thriller, is their fourth book together.

Prologue

*"What would you do if you could foretell the past and the future
of anybody and anything, just with a touch?"*

It is strange how fate ties seemingly arbitrary events together, separated by an indefinite timeline. For Vivaan, this realization would come too soon, and change his life's story forever. His secret ability to foretell the future and the past of any entity by merely a feather touch, would let him seek redemption for a dark past – and deliver him from this stifling burden after a wild journey to free a hauntingly familiar soul.

An automobile engineer by profession, Vivaan lives in London. He spends his busy days building his new automobile powertrain system, and hiding from the world in solace during the night.

Though, destiny being the seductive siren that she is, forces him back to his homeland, India. Leaving his project in the trusted hands of his teammates, Vivaan arrives at the rescue of his ailing father and financially strained family. It is here that he unknowingly befriends the Devil, mesmerized by the big boys' toys he loved so much – cars.

Vivaan's presence in the family stabilizes his family matters for good – but he is soon gripped by unknown visions. He comes across a hauntingly beautiful face that would snatch away his sleep and set him on a journey full of grave threats and revelations. He faces people who are not what they seem, explores foreign lands, and comes across strange findings pertaining to stories of evil, death, destruction, and revenge from the past.

His project is sabotaged, and he almost loses his mind. However,

Vivaan uncovers an old mafia nexus by accident, that would eventually connect the dots for him – as if the past and the future are melding together. Strangely enough, he turns out to be the warrior of a story that started much before his character was even written by fate itself.

Vivaan has too many people to protect and he must move on from his past. He knows too much, and the people he has confronted are cold-blooded. He must face evil – no matter the cost.

Chapter 1

London carried a hint of elegance in its air. Colonial architecture dotted the semi-broad lanes; cafes served anything from greasy to the best fish-n-chips; a churning of a multitude of people always on the move; and a plethora of opportunities that presented itself to the citizens for them to get by. 'Hustle' lay at the heart of the city. This fast-paced rhythmhad the hypnotic power to enable people to dream, chase them, and never settle for less—from the smallest to the biggest. At its core, it was the same for everyone—the drive. This was the thought that crossed Vivaan's mind as he peeped outside, glancing at the busy street below his apartment. Nothing seemed to have changed in the last four years, since he had packed everything and come to London for his higher studies. In actuality, it was this shared quality between the two bustling cities that had made him feel at home, more or less, and reassured him that not much had to change in his life.

The fair-skinned, clean-shaved, athletically built person had been fancied by almost all the eligible girls in the university. His exotic Indian accent worked like a charm on them. His eyes were very lively, but more impressible was the deep love and peace they transmitted to the people he spoke to.

Though, Vivaan had always had a different plan when it came to relationships. He was a stag who stood out, he preferred to stay away from any relationships that could leave him emotionally vulnerable.

Every morning, he would wake up with a heavy, yet intriguing awareness of that reason – a secret he planned to take to his grave. Was it a curse or a boon? 'Mostly a boon,' he would tell himself everyday. However, within him resided a dark mystery from the past.

It had haunted him for years, and he would often find himself alone. He had been a prisoner of this heaviness that restrained him from seizing life since he was 8 years old.

'Some burdens are meant to be borne alone,' he would say to himself. He learned to grow through it eventually. But he never could bury that sad little truth.

But today was different!

Vivaan's research grant, for the fellowship he'd received last year, had been renewed. The last few months were full of passion, sweat, worries, hope and a lot of studies. The team of Mechanical & Automotive Engineers at the University had successfully demonstrated a new 'power-train design' for high-performance SUVs that would consume much less fuel.

Vivaan not only led the team but was the chief designer of this sophisticated mechanism that some world-leading carmakers were now vying to bid for.

'Tik-tik-tik' his alarmclock went on. He lifted his face from the pillow, his eyes half-open. A ray of sunlight came into his room, cutting through a slit between the curtains. His face still digging into the pillow, he snoozed the alarm. It took him another 30 seconds to realize that the Automotive Investors Panel would have already arrived at the university.

Eyes wide open, suddenly he saw clearly. He finished brushing his white teeth and carefully examined his face in the mirror. *Country roads, take me home, to the place, I belong*... his favourite country song would play like a ritual in the background.

'We will do it! Our team will do it. Raptor-M4 will change the way diesel engines are sold,' he mumbled to himself.

Vivaan always preferred to wear black. It was a mystery to everyone in the family as well. 'Why does he always buy & wear black clothes?' they would ask. Another smile crossed his face - 'They think 'this' is a mystery... haha!' For Vivaan, wearing black took the pressure off of thinking of what to wear. 'Black suits every occasion & looks good. Everywhere!' he thought.

That wasn't the whole reason though. The 27-year-old had adapted to remain out of sight over the years. Vivaan preferred not to be noticed. The more eyes on him, the more exposed he felt. It was a deliberate choice.

Drawing his black blazer closer to his body, he looked around the room. Everything seemed to be in order. He shut the music player and one-by-one checked all the taps and appliances—a ritual he liked to follow. Just before stepping out, he quickly checked his reflection: black pants—check, perfectly tied laces on his shiny patent leather shoes—check. Ruffling his hair, he switched off the light and closed the door.

Vivaan entered the common hallway that was lined with a thick, and what was now a greasy dark green velvet carpet. It seemed to make the cramped space for entrances to four other apartments on the floor, even more confining. As he locked his door and put the key in his pocket, he caught a glimpse of something shiny on the dark green floor. He knelt to check it out. 'A ring… Strange,' he mumbled to himself. His fingers instinctively reached out to pick up the small shiny gold band.

As his fingers traced the smooth surface of the ornament, Vivaan's face contorted, his deep-set eyes closed with a force as his thick eyebrows drew in together. Taking in a sharp breath, he stood up as his broad, athletic frame seemed to mechanically unfold. He stared across the hallway with a dead look; it seemed as if he was frozen, and time ceased to exist. Almost a minute passed, and he came back from his trance. Vivaan slipped the ring into his jacket's pocket, turned around and walked towards the lift. 'Mrs. Eleanor shouldn't wear her wedding ring while vacuuming the corridors,' he said to himself.

Chapter 2

The hulking black 15th century-old wrought iron gate seemed to stand guard, welcoming the green electric bike as it whizzed through it. On it, Vivaan adjusted his black blazer as it fluttered in the wind, bringing it closer to his chest. 'So late. Why today!' he cursed angrily. It was a bright sunny morning, and the campus was still calm as a handful of students began entering the premises. Waving at a few, Vivaan swerved his bike to the left, towards the faculty parking spot, halting at his regular spot.

Taking off his helmet and quickly locking it on the stand, he tousled his hair free and ran his hands on his sweaty clean-shaved face. *Okay, almost there. Breathe!* He thought to himself. "Morning, Ed," he greeted the head of campus security with a smile. Edward smiled back. "Mornin' to you! Seems like it gonna be a great day, in nit..."

Vivaan nodded, "Seems so, my man," and ran straight to the lab. He quickly glanced at his digital watch - *9:45 am*, before entering the pristine white door that declared 'Automotive Research' on a small but elegant bronze plaque. The endless expanse of squeaky white floors greeted him, all sound proof, followed by racks of engines on the sides—from ancient to modern, showing the span of human history, sophisticated mechanical parts, blueprints pinned on boards, and board tables as large as two six-seater dining tables combined, scattered with concept models and drawings.

Vivaan placed his bag on a bench and walked over noiselessly to a workbench in the corner, that was occupied by his very punctual team, that was already drowned in the presentation. *The Mecca of Engineering*, he thought to himself. He peered over the people and tried to listen in: "… and by this, we will have successfully demonstrated a new power-train design for high-performance SUVs that would consume much less fuel."

Vivaan mouthed the ending, word-for-word, as his colleague William ended his note. He knew it by heart, knowing they needed to present it before the panel in a couple of hours.

"Morning, Vivaan. Right on time, huh?" Ellie said, looking up and smiling broadly. "Hey," he started with a candid smile. But before he could continue, William, Mahira, Joe and Harrell piped in. "Yep! And we're ready, I guess, for this special morning?" he asked the team.

"The panel is already here. We go in at number 3," Mahira announced. She was not only the head of PR for the team, but was also a true friend of Vivaan. Coming from Nagpur, she was someone who had made him feel at home when he was new to the city.

"So Vivaan, we've been through the 3-D model, the projection…" Ellie tallied the checklist. Vivaan settled in his chair, and Mahira noticed how Ellie put his lab coat away, pulled a chair close to his and sat down. Rolling her eyes, Mahira went back to her planner.

Ellie narrated from her checklist and as she came to a close, she untied her hair, letting it fall over her shoulders. "Do you want to grab a coffee?" she asked, catching his eye.

"Umm, not really, I just had tea and…"

Vivaan started but Ellie cut him off before he could finish. "Oh, it's okay, no biggie. But you can help me get around this gearbox layout, right? It would really help…" she said, her deep blue eyes large and pleading as she spoke.

"Hmm… Well… Let me see," replied Vivaan as he bent forward and took the tablet from her, gently caressing her fingers with his.

Ellie blushed. *It is finally coming together*, she yelped inside as she gazed at the man whom she had fancied since the beginning of the *Raptor-M4* project.

Ellie waited for Vivaan to say something. To her, it seemed like he was lost figuring out the contents on the screen, but something else seemed to have happened. Vivaan wasn't stirring. He seemed to have gone into a trance, his body suddenly rigid. Mahira, who had been sitting across, noticed the change in her friend's demeanour. After all, she had seen this for years now...

Vivaan came out of the trance suddenly. Ellie was too busy fantasizing about him and didn't notice anything odd.

He subtly gulped down his saliva, handed over the tablet to Ellie and got up awkwardly. He tried to make an excuse. Ellie looked at him, sensing that something wasn't right. "I shall be back in a minute," he said, and he went towards the door with an expressionless face.

"Hey, Harrell, could you please wind up faster? The panel might begin any moment… I'll just be back," said Mahira and hurried out of the lab.

Joe noticed Mahira as she went away. "No chance, mate," laughed William. "She is way more mature than you, bruv. *And* you are just an intern!"

Ellie couldn't bear William's words. She got up and stormed off the lab.

They noticed her odd behaviour. "What happened to her?"

***

The large, hulking auditorium could hold up to 500 people at once. Its walls were decorated with red velvet curtains lined with golden frills and threading that gave the impression of an ancient opera house. The ceiling seemed endless, and the stage, some 2 feet high, could make anyone nervous, and that was where the panel of four investors sat in front of a collapsible table and chairs.

Designers of the RAPTOR-M4 System walked in a single file with Vivaan in the middle, his hands rested inside his black trouser pockets. "So, as decided, I will talk about the production viability..." he started. Mahira smiled, "Don't worry. We've practiced this like a million times now."

Penny Rubin, the one in charge of student affairs came onto the podium on the stage. "Good morning, fellow scientists. As I can see the teams have all joined us, so let us proceed," she smiled, looking at the students. "Today we have the honour of having our esteemed panel here. They are all pioneers in the automotive industry in the United Kingdom, and they need no introduction. So please extend a warm welcome to Ms Gleah Navarro, Mr Avington John, Mr Raymond Takahashi and Mr Sandeep Cherian here with us. Welcome,panellists!"

A smattering of claps and cheers went up the audience. Penny raised her hand. "As we all know, the teams will present and the investors here will vote and then pledge their investment for the most viable projects. To secure this, a team needs a minimum of 2 votes from the panellists and a fair agreement on the funding details. So now we have that out of the way..."

The hall filled with thunderous applause. "The session will commence in 5-minutes," Penny announced with a smile.

Vivaan sat at the table with a Zen face. He turned to his right to look at Mahira. "Well, I guess this is the big moment?" he asked sipping water from a bottle. Mahira squeezed his free hand and smiled just as Ellie caught his eye and rolled hers, turning away.

In the background, Penny's soft voice reverberated through the speakers: "And now! Our first team for the day. Let's welcome Dr Olson and his engineers."

***

By now Vivaan had walked in and out of the auditorium several times in the past ninety minutes. As he paced frantically, to and fro in the corridor yet again, Mahira walked out. "Are you okay?" she asked. Vivaan, oblivious to her words, kept ruffling his hair and looking at the ceiling absent-mindedly. "Vivaan... Are you okay?" she asked, now a little louder.

"Oh... What?"

"Is it about the pitch, Vivaan? Are you nervous?"

Vivaan shook his head. "No, no... Nothing! Let us go inside. Sorry, M," he said, giving her a half-hug. Mahira forced a smile; in all the years of knowing him, sometimes Vivaan would act strangely, and though she would try to ask him, he had always been guarded. "Yeah, sure," she replied, knowing that today too her questions would come back unanswered, just like they had in the morning when he had walked out of the lab.

***

"Mr Vivaan Anand and his team of engineers will present their revolutionary power-train design now," Penny announced, as Ellie, Harrell and Mahira walked up to the stage.

Mahira took over the mic, "I hope the panel and all the attendees are having a fine morning. Today, I would like to introduce you all to the new *Raptor-M4* power-train design for mid-sized and large SUVs. What is it? How is it going to change the performance design of SUVs forever? For that, I would ask my colleague Ellie to take the mic," she cued Ellie towards the podium.

As Ellie walked to the podium, Mahira stepped back and triggered her laser-pointer to the large projector screen adjacent to the panel seating and the audience.

Vivaan laid back on his chair, Harrell and Joe waited for their part, while William worked backstage to ensure a smooth operation.

The session finally began!

"As we know, modern SUV power suffers high losses in terms of friction. They are heavy and operate in high-load conditions that also increase their wear and tear," Ellie started smoothly. The animation played on the projection as she spoke.

"To the carmakers, that means loss of fuel efficiency and high cost of manufacturing. And to the car-owners, it means a higher cost of maintenance and fuel. Our design aims to solve it all..." Ellie continued. By now, the panel was gripped by the compelling 3-D film of the design that played in the backdrop.

"I would like to introduce you to the new *Raptor-M4* Power-Train," as Ellie finally unveiled the design, Vivaan's eye went towards the impeccably dressed icon of automation, Glean Navarro, who sat alert now. Her eyes peered at the screen like an eagle.

Vivaan noticed Navarro's interest as Ellie continued to drive the pitch. "...So, the rolling tension is minimized, and the power reaching the drive-shaft is boosted by 9%. The result? Higher traction on-demand, efficient engine performance and lower..." Before Ellie could finish, Gleah motioned for a question.

"And how does the transmission unit calculate the number of switches to be made between the rails of the shaft? Not to mention the minute stress calculations that change every fraction of a second?" Gleah asked with an uninterested air, fiddling with her pen that reflected in her hawk-like eyes.

But the team was already prepared for this, and by the time Gleah posed her question, Mahira had already cued Ellie to call Harrell.

"I would like my colleague Mr. Harrell O'Neal to answer that for you, Ms Navarro," Ellie quipped as Gleah kept staring, her pen still dancing between her fingers.

Harrell got up and dove straight to the answer–just like they had prepared in previous rehearsals—it was a cakewalk.

"The variomatic transmission chip will also calculate the change in load conditions for the shaft, thereby, switching between the rails in real-time...." By the time Harrell sat back down, everyone on the team had smiles on their faces.

Vivaan looked at Gleah Navarro, who seemed impassive. Though she sat like a cold and expressionless figurine made of wood, Vivaan had a strong hunch that the team had already sold the design.

They had won the day. That look of Zen on Vivaan's face was rare as far as Mahira knew. The pitches were over, and it was lunchtime – an opportunity for the team to have a word with the investors 'informally.'

Chapter 3

The university band played Bach's *Sonata Number 5* in the background, all dressed in their band uniforms and lined up like dolls at the other end of the dining hall that supported a 20-feet high roof on its twelve elegantly decorated pillars. The walls, lined with old Renaissance-era paintings and oil-on-canvas portraits of the university's founding fathers, projected an authoritative air which was very much the intention.

Vivaan, Mahira and Harrell stood with glasses of white wine, barely sipping out of them, looking anxiously around the room that was hosting the meet-and-greet for the panel and the teams. Everyone in the university knew it was less to do with lunch and more to do with networking; trying to sway the panel that was making their decisions on the funding.

"Where *are* those two?" Vivaan asked, his eyes scanning for his other teammates across the crowded room.

"Probably loading their plates with food!" Harrell rolled his eyes.

As if on cue, Joe and Williams appeared from behind the rest. "Who? Who are we talking about, bruv?" said William, balancing his plate of overloaded food from the buffet.

"Go easy! That's a lot of carbs," laughed Harrell, continuing, "Wasn't Ellie with you?"

"Oh guys, here she comes," Mahira quipped, her brown eyes fixed at the entrance to the hall. She then turned towards Vivaan, who couldn't seem to take his eyes off the woman who had entered the room.

"Isn't she too old for you, Vivaan?" Mahira teased him, eyeing the sophisticated frame of Gleah Navarro.

Vivaan laughed aloud as if caught. "Nah! She is a vision!" Vivaan winked. Mahira smiled to herself. She liked this easy-going version of her friend who sometimes seemed vague and lost, his shoulders too heavy with God-knows-what.

"Do you think she will just walk up to us and offer us money? That'll be fun, right?" Mahira asked.

"Well, who knows, my friend. But I know one thing—for that you'll have to initiate the conversation. Because you are so natural at networking," Vivaan said, taking a sip of wine.

Mahira rolled her eyes. "Alright, fine! I know a hint when it stares at my face. Wish me luck," she said, running her fingers down her brown tresses that she'd now opened up. Practising her best smile and the wine glass placed firmly in one hand, she confidently sashayed, navigating the crowd deftly, straight towards the legendary Gleah Navarro.

Joe and Williams looked at Mahira with awe as they saw her offering a helping hand to the scion at the salad bar, smiling. "Every single time! How does she do that?" asked William. "It's crazy insane. She's got a gift."

"Well, let's hope the gift works in our favour," added Joe.

After what seemed like hours, Mahira traced her path back with a cheetah-like attitude to the corner where the team now stood. She locked eyes with Vivaan as she came closer.

Vivaan started laughing.

"What? What? Well?" hammered Joe at the back.

"Oh, c'mon, just tell us now. I hate it when you guys do this telepathy thing," Harrell grunted.

"I think you already know the answer," came the reply as Vivaan tipped his wine glass to his oldest friend.

***

It was past eleven in the night. The curtain fluttered open, drawing Vivaan to peer outside his apartment. The streetlights shimmered on the road and the scattered water puddles. A few cars were parked on the curb and *Sandwich Bar* was still open with its blue-green neon sign flickering in the dark on an almostdeserted street. Sealing his windowpane, Vivaan drew the curtains wide open.

He dialled a number on his phone and waited for a response from the other end. "Oh, hey! When are you gonna be here?" He peeked outside the window again. "See you at the sandwich bar then? Sure thing," he said, grabbing his jacket and hurrying downstairs.

As he walked out of his building, he saw Mahira's frame getting out of her car. Her heavy grey overcoat and brown hair, now coloured, in the blue-green of the neon sign.

"So, the regular? And a Soda?"

"Yes. And a smoke as well," Mahira said, breathing hard. "Long day, man."

The couple began walking, lost in the melting flavours of the best sandwich in the city; cool breeze melded with peace caressed their faces.

"So, any follow-up on Gleah?" Vivaan asked.

"Umm," Mahira lit her thin, filtered cigarette, taking a long drag. "Yeah, actually. So, she has invited the team to her office on Friday to sign an MoU."

"Memorandum of Understanding so quickly?" replied Vivaan, while taking their regular order from the shop window. "Hmm… So, you talked about our funding and credit conditions?" he asked, walking ahead to their usual bench where they had spent countless evenings.

Mahira nodded as she bit into her sandwich. "Boy, this is as good as ever! Yeah… so, Gleah seems to have no problems with our conditions and –" but before she could complete her sentence, Vivaan drew her in for a hug. The hug was warm and felt relaxed and comforting.

"Aww… c'mon," Mahira blushed. "There is no need. This is for all of us," she laughed.

The night drew on as the two finished their sandwiches. Vivaan fiddled for the lighter in his pocket. He lit hers and then his.

"Vivaan, would you mind if I asked you something?" Mahira said inhaling.

"Of course not. Why do you even ask?"

"Well, it is personal so… I don't want to… you know, encroach."

"Hmm... I guess we have been friends for the longest. Ask. Please."

"What do you keep thinking... like, you go into these strange moods... I'm worried for you," she said, locking eyes with him.

"Thinking? I don't... What strange moods? I don't get it?" he said, steering away and looking down the dusty street.

"Oh c'mon. You just said we've been friends for over 5 years. I do recognize patterns, Vivaan. We're all scientists after all. And I know you know what I am talking about. I'm just worried for you because the frequency of these moods has increased over the last few years. You have to tell me *now*," she finished, firmly.

Seconds of silence prevailed between the two.

Vivaan took a deep breath, then leaned back on the bench, giving up. In all these years he had known Mahira, she had never pried into something he didn't want her to.

"Can I trust you?" he sighed.

Mahira gave a perplexed look. "Of course. You are talking as if you don't know me."

"Well... Umm... The thing is," Vivaan stammered, playing with the cigarette butt. "I haven't told this to anyone... But yeah, lately it's been getting too much I guess..." he continued, "... and... and I don't know... It is a secret I have kept hidden from the world. Even from my family..."

Mahira got a little tense, her legs snug together and she crossed her arms as she took a deep drag. "What is it?"

"I have a special... umm, well, you can say *ability*," Vivaan said looking at the ground in front of him, trying to keep calm. The last thing he would want was to sound like a lunatic to his most trusted friend.

Mahira turned towards him, her eyes seemed to bore into his face. "Look at me, Vivaan."

Vivaan turned to her slowly, his eyes a little watery. "Mahira, you may think me mad, but the plain truth is that sometimes I can see the past and the future… of… of a person or even an object by just a touch. It's umm… well, I say a gift maybe… I dunno…" he trailed off.

Mahira drew in a sharp breath. "So… you touch things, and you see what happens?" She said without blinking.

"Yeah… So, basically, I can just touch and know a lot about anything," he said, now looking at the stars in the sky.

"You know, Vivaan, you could have said no I don't want to tell you Mahira, instead of this cooked-up story. I thought we were friends. But this joke…" Mahira started to get up, her face red and contorted. "Listen Vivaan. I never judge, least of all you. But it seems our friendship was based on flimsy—"

"Your dad gifted you this overcoat." Vivaan interrupted. "His last gift to you before he died. It was 9 years ago. You still use it because it feels like he's still here, with you, like he never left you. But it also acts as a reminder that love can disappear away anytime. That is why you never fall for anyone."

Vivaan was taken aback; it was like a barrage had opened and the water was now gushing out.

What followed was a long silence. Mahira's eyes deluged with tears, stayed put on the street beneath her feet. "I'm… I'm sorry—" Vivaan now began regretting his confession, but suddenly Mahira came rushing and hugged him tightly.

The sudden vibration and loud voice of John Denver through Vivaan's cell phone tore through the deafening silence.

"Yeah, *ma*?" Vivaan spoke, clicking on the screen as Mahira looked at her watch questioningly; after all, it was too late to call.

"What... Slow down. Slow down, *ma*," Vivaan's voice seemed to be breaking.

He took a deep breath to calm his senses. "I will be home on the next flight. Don't worry. I'll be there soon," he said hanging up, his head in his hands.

"What happened?"

"Dad... He suffered a cardiac arrest. I need to leave for India tonight," he said, looking at the dark end of the street.

Chapter 4

Vivaan had never been extravagant when it came to life's comforts. In fact, he was overtly modest when it came to splurging on himself. But there was only one fast flight from Heathrow to Mumbai, and the only one with a few Business Class seats left unoccupied. Hence, Vivaan had no choice. As the airliner scrambled at 38,000 feet, Vivaan glanced at his watch that read: 4:00. Almost all the cabin lights were off, and the mild humming sound of the engines made for a great white noise for his fellow passengers to fall asleep to.

But as sleep remained elusive, Vivaan traced the white sheets of clouds that danced against the fading darkness of the breaking dawn. Gazing at the infinite sky and the uncanny calm outside the small window, he turned to his watch again when out of nowhere, an irritated sound cracked the silence, "Yeah! 10 more hours to go. Now if you could please stop looking at the watch." Vivaan turned to his side; it was the pot-bellied man sitting next to him, who was rolling his eyes and looking agitated. For a minute or two Vivaan was perplexed by the man's comment but chose not to speak. He did, however, give him a look that lasted a moment longer than necessary.

He dove back into his make-believe conversation with his dad.

'Dad... you must be kidding me. I want you to play with your grandkids. I am sure you are not taking enough rest. Maybe you are eating too much with Rustom Uncle. That is it! You don't listen. You never listen. Vidya will probably say yes to marriage soon. Who will handle all that?'

Watching the dark clouds outside brought about a certain heaviness inside Vivaan, and suddenly he felt uneasy. Pressing the button overhead, he called for the stewardess. In barely a few seconds, a petite girl with a ready smile walked to his row. Sensing the interference, the pot-bellied man's snoring stopped suddenly. He opened his eyes and groaned to indicate his sleep had been disturbed again but seeing the hostess he calmed down.

"How may I help you, sir?" she whispered to Vivaan.

"Can I get some... chocolates please?" Vivaan asked.

"Chocolates. Right. Any preferences?"

Vivaan shook his head and smiled. The hostess reciprocated with a nod and left, only to quickly return with a tray containing an array of nuggets. All this while Vivaan noticed the man next to him eyeing the girl. "Do you want something too?" he asked a little too aggressively as the man enlarged his eyes at the young man's insolence and went back to sleep.

She was somehow pleased to serve him. Vivaan looked out. The sun was about to rise to welcome another day.

After a few hours of broken sleep, he finally awoke to a bustle in the cabin. And light!

His head wasn't at its best, but he was fine with it. An aspirin would have done. But he chose not to have one. He looked at the obnoxious man beside him. He was reading some stocks magazine that rested on his well-rounded belly. Vivaan was amazed at how round it was.

The fat man looked at Vivaan again despite his best intentions to go undetected. His almost-bald head shone under the cabin light, his eye-movements were funny. His smile was even funnier because it revealed two missing center teeth from his lower jaw. That elicited a smile on Vivaan's face. The fat man was slightly puzzled and embarrassed. He dove back into his magazine again.

Vivaan decided to update Mahira about his journey. Though he couldn't make a call in front of his fellow passengers. He pulled his cozy blanket aside, refreshed his eyes and made a gesture to move out of the seat.

With a little disturbance and without grabbing much attention to his movements, he stood in the middle of an open aisle.

Vivaan walked straight towards the lavatory. It was occupied so he decided to wait close to the pantry shelf. He wanted to make a call but was unsure if he could. A stewardess walked in at that moment. Vivaan was busy playing with his phone. "Sir, may I help you?"

He immediately recognized the voice. A sigh of relief settled on his face. He smiled again at her. "Yes!" and both chuckled. He motioned for a handshake and introduced himself to the sweet stewardess. "I am Natasha," she said as her eyes pierced his soul with ethereal sweetness.

"Natasha. You saved my night with chocolates. Thanks a lot for that."

"Always happy to serve you, sir!"

"Not sir. Vivaan. I insist." Natasha adjusted her hair, and her smile brightened her face.

"Sure, Vivaan."

"So, Natasha. I have been wanting to make an urgent call to my colleague. Can I please do that?"

Natasha looked at him as if she had caught him in his over-smart trick of 'being charming and nice' to women.

Natasha smiled again. "But... only one quick call, Vivaan."

He gave her a big monkey smile and thanked her. He then called Mahira.

"...Sure. I know you will handle everything there. I don't know how long I will be in India. We will be in touch," Vivaan said.

"No worries. I am here. You take care of the family," Mahira said from the other side.

"Hey... Mahira! Thanks. Thanks for being there..." he said to her.

"For you, always," she said.

The lavatory was vacant now. But, Mahira's voice had sent him into another mental mystery. Somehow, he was missing her in a way he never had before. He was in the midst of mental-roller-coaster thoughts as he went back to his seat. Vivaan's train of thoughts only derailed when he came across the fat man shouting at someone on his phone, probably on the call or text service that was allowed on the airline.

The words he spoke were disgusting. The way he spoke was abhorrent. He was talking to his wife.

"Oh! Oh! Now you want the money, you bi**h. You got the children and now you want the money, too?" The man suddenly came out, panting. As he saw Vivaan he froze, and then picked up pace and walked towards his seat hurriedly.

A while later, Vivaan walked back. The man paid no attention to his arrival; he was still red and sweaty because of the argument. Unbeknownst to him that his neighbor was watching, he took out a small blue towel from a brown bag and wiped his face, breathing in hard... He still struggled to breathe as Vivaan decided to interrupt.

"Chocolate might help," he said, taking one out from his pocket. The man looked at him and sheepishly took it.

Vivaan sank back into the seat. "Don't want to, but that was some bitter conversation..." he said.

"That is what happens when you're married, I guess," spoke the man. "That woman has made this marriage tiring. She has made me too tired," the man sighed.

Vivaan nodded. He thought it would be better to be receptive to whatever words were coming out of the man's mouth. "Hmm... It's always two-sided. Give and receive. Help and be helped. May I know what happened... If you don't mind?"

The man looked at Vivaan for a moment. "Hmm... Yeah! Maybe talking will help me... That was my wife. She divorced me last year. The children went with her. Now she wants more alimony... More than before, says she need it for tuitions and the kids, and I don't even see them."

"Hmm... So, you still love your family?"

The man looked at him quizzically, and then turned his gaze

away. He stared into oblivion. Nobody had asked him this question in years; everything was just bitterness and anger. He broke his silence: "Of course. I did love them."

"*Did?*"

"Did… Do. I mean I do, still," he said, almost embarrassed.

"Maybe reach out to them genuinely then. Nothing is completely broken. You just need to make amends, I guess. Let go of the bitterness."

A long silence followed.

"What do you do, by the way?" Vivaan asked, picking up a magazine from the retractable holder in front.

"Investment banker."

"Oh! That's great."

The man smiled and extended his hand to Vivaan. "Dilip. Dilip Poonawalla."

"I am Vivaan Anand."

Things were better for the rest of the flight as some sort of warmth entered the interaction between the flight's neighbors. Vivaan felt a little better too, knowing that the man's heart was somehow lightened.

At 3:00 pm, the jet touched the runway at Mumbai airport. As he collected his luggage, Vivaan saw Dilip again.

"Listen, I apologize… my behaviour—" began Dilip, just as Vivaan interrupted him. He first put his hand on his shoulder, but then decided to hug him. This puzzled Dilip.

"Just two things. Stop smoking and know this, your wife, and kids… they miss you. You don't need more money to hoard. You need more love. Have a good life!" Vivaan said as he hurried out to catch a cab.

Perplexed but greatly moved, Dilip saw him off.

***

The roads were soaked. Puddles were everywhere as tyres stomped and splashed on them. Mumbai's rain was the same as ever. Vivaan was mesmerized by the ever-bustling streets of Mumbai: the old Church Road, the cinema complex, that beach spot with sumptuous street food lined up—all those places where he'd once wandered as if tomorrow didn't matter.

His cab came to a stop opposite a big building with a humongous red-cross sign. Vivaan stepped out of the cab as the rain drizzled down on him. He smiled; he felt that the city was welcoming him in its own way. "I am here to see Mr. Rishi Anand, and if you could point me to the luggage room, if you have one," he said to the nurse at the reception.

As he moved through the overly pristine hallways deluged with the smell of medicines, childhood memories that particularly haunted him came rushing in. Just then, he thought he saw a familiar figure at a distance. There was a momentary pause between the two – after all, it had been 3 years since Vivaan had last come to India.

"Vivaan!"

"Chikoo?" Vivaan exclaimed as he sped towards him.

"C'mon. Not in front of people, I've told you!" Raunak laughed as he pulled Vivaan in for a hug. "*Tu nahi sudhrega…*"

"So, your dad came out of surgery an hour ago. Doctors say things will be fine but he's under stress. Your mom was saying something about the business... Anyway, that's for later. Have lunch. I was just about to join your mom and Vidya for lunch in the cafeteria downstairs," Raunak explained as they walked.

Vivaan saw his mother from a distance; Amrita Anand was clad in an orange saree. She was seated at the table in the corner. Looking at her only son walking over, she stood up and started crying, overwhelmed. Vivaan hugged her, tearing up. Taking a deep breath, he kissed his mother's forehead.

"I am so glad you are here, Vivaan," his mother's throat couldn't bear the heaviness of the emotions, though her somber face was at ease now.

"Vivaan!" Vidya came forward, carrying a try of food. Keeping it down, she gave him a tight hug. "We missed you so much," she sighed.

"So did I, kid!" he ruffled the hair of his pampered sister who held the secrets to his love life, fears, and ambitions.

While eating, Vivaan inquired, "Why is dad under stress? He never tells me anything."

"You know how he is," his mom gave a sad smile. "His attitude is not really helping. The Doctor says stress is bad for him. But stress is the only thing he knows," she said tearing up.

"I'll talk to him. You all don't have to worry anymore."

***

It was 9 pm and the streets of Mumbai glittered, bathed in lights from buildings and houses and vehicles passing by. Vivaan and Raunak sat in the hospital cafeteria, catching up over coffee. After many pleadings, he had managed to send his mother and sister home to rest.

As they sipped the piping hot and mildly brewed coffee, Raunak spoke up, "Something seems to be off with your dad. I am not sure what... And I didn't want to say anything in front of your mom."

Vivaan gave him a puzzled look. "Off? In what way?"

"Don't know. Your mom says he had been throwing huge tantrums for the last couple of days. And he won't say why. But, even to me, as I met him some days back while shopping... He is not the same anymore..."

"Hmm... Let's walk to his room."

As they walked out of the lift, Vivaan stayed quiet. His dad had always been a happy-go-lucky man and was usually cheerful. Even on calls he couldn't picture him sad or worried. But this news was a revelation.

They looked through the circular glass window of room number 117. Raunak stopped. "Hey... I'd rather stay here. You meet him." Vivaan nodded and entered.

There he lay on the large white bed, all the monitors and drips working around him. His beard was overgrown, his hair as white as snow, yet his moustache still royal. Vivaan couldn't remember so many wrinkles on his face. His old man had grown older. *'I never thought he would get old and vulnerable like this.'* He went closer to him.

His dad opened his eyes only after he pulled a small chair close to him. His head rolled towards him as Vivaan grabbed his hand and pacified it with as much affection God gave him. For the first time, he saw tears roll down his eyes.

"Dad... It is fine. I am here," Vivaan said. Though, it wasn't just the words that he spoke for reassurance. Even before his father could move his lips to articulate a meaningful word, Vivaan caught a glimpse of his dad's actual troubles.

One touch was all it took for Vivaan to trace the past and the future through his father's eyes. He zoned-out and came back – as if someone had jolted him out of a daydream. He could now understand what was actually troubling his dad.

"I have been waiting for you for so long. I am sorry you have to see me like this..." his dad said.

Vivaan just nodded. He just wanted to listen. He just wanted to see if his dad would share his burdens with him.

"Your presence is so wonderful. Now I can get out of this God-forsaken hospital tomorrow."

Vivaan smiled. "You are not going anywhere unless the doctors say so."

"Oh! I am fine. Your mom and sister and the doctors, they worry unnecessarily. You don't know these hospital people. They just want money." Vivaan could see his dad's tantrum manifest.

"Dad! There is no arguing with that. Okay?"

After what seemed like a while, his father spoke. "There is something I want to tell you, Vivaan," his voice cracked.

Vivaan leaned closer to him. He knew what he would say. He wanted to listen anyway.

"Things... Things are bad here."

"Bad?"

His dad nodded."Business is in loss. Debt has taken over all our savings. I owe a lot to a lot of people," dad revealed. "Your sister is to marry shortly. I know she likes a guy... good family and all. But it seems like time has turned against me," he almost wept.

Vivaan took his dad's hand in his palm. "You could've told me this before, Dad."

"I... I..." the old man started but broke down again.

"Don't worry, now. We are all together. You can be in peace now. No stress and no temper! I will make things right for you," he sighed as he held his father's hand tightly.

Chapter 5

Every step they took left an impression in the wet sand. The waves would wash some of them away, leaving some to exist. Vivaan was lost in his thoughts, looking at the water caressing his feet and moving away. "Vivaan," spoke up Raunak. He wasn't used to this new quiet version of his best buddy. He had only known a cheerful Vivaan, who he had known forever now. But Vivaan didn't seem to hear. The sea breeze caressed their faces.

Raunak asked, "Well? What did you and your dad talk about? You've been quiet since." Still, Vivaan seemed too lost to notice the words.

"Vivaan! Bro!"

Vivaan jerked out of his stupor and looked up. His cigarette had almost reached the butt and he had barely taken a puff. "Damn...," he said, throwing it away from the water, towards the beach.

"Tell! What's happened to you? Just say it. Whatever it is!" Raunak insisted.

Vivaan hesitated for a while, then seeing a *pani puri* stall at a distance, proposed a quick snack. Raunak caught his shift. "This won't change the conversation you know. I will not drop it till you tell me."

It wasn't the tidiest eating counter at the beach. Though, *panipuri* lovers care less about the tidiness. As the stall operator prepared plates for his new visitors, Vivaan was back in his train of thoughts. "Vivaan, *yaar!*" Raunak didn't have enough patience.

"What?"

Raunak raised his brows and asked him again "What's wrong with you?" Vivaan took a deep breath and shook his head firmly, with a small, forced smile on his face. "It really is nothing... Just putting a few things together. Really."

Before the conversation could continue, the teenaged *panipuri-*wala offered them loaded plates of the sumptuous delicacy. Raunak grabbed his plate and dashed those snacks straight into his mouth. Vivaan was astonished - "You are a genuine foody!" he chuckled. "And you care that I am no longer paying attention to your odd silence." They both shared a laugh. The breeze felt even betternow.

"Hmm... well, so... I should tell mom that you have a girlfriend now. She has been wondering if you are still single," Raunak laughed out loud.

"Really?" Vivaan couldn't hide his sarcasm.

His worries faded away as the night fell upon the city. A good night's sleep was all he required. He wondered what it would be like to sleep in his old room once again, relive those memories again. Somewhere, beyond all the troubles of the world, he had found a reason to be happy in his home again. Little did he know that trouble would become his shadow, for a long time to come.

***

It was a week later that the doctors allowed Rishi Anand to be discharged from the hospital. With strict recommendations and a long list of medicines, they advised him not to get stressed or angry. As Vivaan and Raunak sat him in the car, his eyes gleamed with the bright morning light.

"You finally happy, dad?" Vivaan turned around to glance at his father enjoying a taste of the outside world.

Rishi was busy peeping out the car window as he murmured under his breath - "Oh! I was always happy. Life it is…" he trailed off, brushing a tear away. Raunak and Vivaan exchanged a brief look.

"Don't worry. Everything is fine now, uncle. Everyone is waiting for you at home," said Raunak as he started the engine.

The car picked up the pace and combed through the now-filtering traffic of the morning. The palms lined on the side and the hawkers setting up shop added to the peaceful silence in the car. Vivaan leaned his head out of the window, eyeing the old bakery where he would buy cupcakes after school, every day, like a set ritual. The old red-brick colonial bungalows followed next, each with its own little ornamental garden in the front. Vivaan smiled. *Things never change,* he thought to himself as he now drove past the old park where he would play football with his friends, many of whom he had lost touch with. He then saw an old lady watering some pots kept at her wide but short wrought-iron gate. "God! Is that Mrs. Desai?" Vivaan asked, pointing backwards as the car sped away. "Haha! You recognize her? She seems to be getting on with age…" his father said.

"Yeah, of course. No one can forget her and her house."

"Remember she used to make us all lemonade when we returned home after a tiring evening?" Raunak asked, as his hands turned the steering to the left towards a narrow road.

"Yeah, sweet and salty with those jam biscuits... Seems like ages have gone by," Vivaan smiled as the nostalgic visions flashed through his mind.

The car stopped in front of a white two-storied house. Its roof was covered with a beautiful pattern of red bricks laid in a zig-zag fashion. The gate was studded with creepers and climbers, and the boundary walls hosted a show of flowerpots and bird feeders. As the car entered the driveway, Vivaan saw the mango tree right in the middle of the small garden near the patio, which also housed a small pond.

The two friends got Rishi out of the car and into the house, where everyone in the family was waiting for him. After settling Rishi in his room and while bidding goodbye to Vivaan's mom, Raunak turned to his friend, who mouthed: "'Thank you" and a gentle bow. Raunak, rolling his eyes, waved it off.

Half hugging him as he entered the car, Raunak looked up at Vivaan. "You still haven't told me what you two spoke about... I'll be waiting," he winked and drove off.

Vivaan smiled and waved him off, and walked back in, to his mother who waited at the door. "Let's eat. You must be hungry, *beta*."

Vivaan chuckled as he folded his sleeves and dove right into his favourite *poori bhaji* that his mother served him.

"Hey! *Maa*, is my room in the same shape I had left it?" Vivaan evaluated his mother's reaction. Before she could utter a word, Vidya poked in their conversation from nowhere - "Sorry brother! Your room is mine now," and she ran away. Vivaan almost caught her.

"C'mon you guys. Let your dad sleep. Vivaan, come, let us have dinner. Vidu is just teasing," mom said.

"Ya, that is the problem," Vivaan naughtily conspired with mom. His little sister showed him a monkey face and disappeared.

At the dinner table, as they all ate, the atmosphere became heavy with emotion; after all, it was after a considerable number of years that the family was together again. "You don't get enough of Indian food in London, I guess, do you Vivaan?" Amrita Anand inquired.

"Oh! No, no. There is an Indian restaurant. In fact, a *Punjabi* restaurant near the corner where I live. Recently opened. Mahira and I often go there when we feel homesick," Vivaan spoke as he licked his fingers clean of the finest curry.

"Oh! Mahira? Is that the same girl..." his mother began, but Vivaan was too busy eating the food he'd missed all these years.

"Haan, *maa*. Mahira. I told you about her on the phone. Remember she was there when we had that video call?" "Oh! *Achcha*..." his mom mouthed as she strained to remember.

Vivaan's chewing halted. He looked at them both and gave a confused but embarrassed laugh. "No! No! No... It is not like that... We're... we are great friends," he said reaching for the glass of water as he saw his mom's eyebrow rise. "C'mon *maa*! Please," he laughed.

Anand family's dining hall seemed to have come alive after a long time. And as he laughed, Vivaan's eyes stopped at a picture that decorated the grey-green wall, right beside the kitchen. In it was a pretty girl with black hair and big shiny eyes and wheat-coloured skin. She resembled Vidya in all ways. Though, she looked like a teen. Her smile was colourful and full of life. Just like the fresh garland of flowers that surrounded her portrait.

***

It was a calm night, and everybody had gone to sleep except Vivaan who absent-mindedly strummed his guitar. *'Don't all happy memories seem like a fairytale?'* he asked himself as his fingers plucked at the strings. *'Why doesn't every passing moment seem special then? Or do we miss the important stuff, and we never learn?'* He stretched his back and closed his eyes, half-lying on the bed. But sleep was still distant.

He rose from the bed and walked over to the window, leaning on the ledge. The gently swaying palms caught his attention. Vivaan looked up and noticed the sheets of clouds, dry and incapable of bearing rumbling thunder. He fished out his phone and thought of ringing Raunak. After a second, he threw the phone on the bed, changing his mind.

He was just having second thoughts when suddenly the phone rang.

"Hey! I'm okay, Mahira. So glad you called. I was thinking of you," he spoke, half whispering, aware that everyone was asleep.

"Vivaan, are you alone?" Mahira asked.

"Yes, why?"

"How is your dad?"

"He is fine. We got him home today. Mahira, you sound a little…"

"Yeah… Umm… I've been wanting to tell you this but didn't want to bother you and message…"

"What is it?"

"Well, the thing is… Gleah backed off from the deal. Our project has no investor now."

Silence seemed to shadow everything suddenly.

"Vivaan, you there?"

Vivaan cleared his throat. "Yeah… But I don't get it. Everything was fine. What happened?"

Mahira's deep sigh could be heard over the speaker. "Listen. I am not sure about this, but there seems to be an industry shark behind this."

"A what?"

"Yeah. It's skewed. The… monopoly or some mafia-style deal has taken over our design. Vivaan, this seems scary. I tried reaching out to a couple of investors. They are not even picking up our calls…"

Silence prevailed again.

"Okay. Umm… Let me think. You take care… and listen, Mahira, please stay in touch with the team."

He leaned against the window and observed the cityscape in the dead of the night. The clouds had now turned frothy, dark, and grey. Vivaan looked at the leaves on the palm that has caught his attention earlier, just as heavy rain droplets rolled down them like shining pearls.

Chapter 6

It was a long night for Vivaan. Sleep eluded him for most of the hours. Then, he woke up before everyone else to take his favourite car for a spin.

Vivaan walked down the stairs in his pyjamas, his eyes a little puffy, and his hair like a cuckoo's nest. At the end of the main compound, a white steel shutter covered the garage. Vivaan walked up and unbolted it to push the shutter up. There stood his favourite beauty, wrapped in a silver cover. He pulled it off with a flourish – almost with a magician's pride in his eyes.

The Jeep was a little dusty but in perfectly restored condition. *'Dad took good care of it,'* he thought, as he took out the jingling keys from his pocket and sat in.

As soon as he grabbed the steering wheel, all the good ol' memories overwhelmed his mind. He shifted the heavy yet sporty transmission into reverse. The battle-green open Jeep began to roll back and exited the house gate. Vidya saw his brother drive away.

***

The real fun of driving the old Willys was at about 30 kmph. Feeling its roaring sound through the gearshift added to the fun. A few minutes later, he didn't realize he had arrived at the main road. He pulled over and idled the engine with the sweet melody of pistons and shafts operating under burning fuel.

He looked across the road. A bright whiteboard with red letters and graffiti red – *Uncle Sam's Fish & Chips*. The shutter was already up and there was movement in the shop. Vivaan almost stepped out of the car, but then stopped and retracted his leg back in. His dad's business was a few kilometers ahead, on the same road. He decided to stop by and take a look at it.

The engine roared back, and the Jeep sped away.

Vivaan arrived in the commercial area of *Maratha Global* market. Most of the shops were closed and there was hardly any human presence. He slid the Jeep into a narrow concrete patch beside the road and found himself standing in front of a 5-floor high, glass-studded building with all kinds of businesses. Amidst the crowd of billboards, ads, banners and large LED screens, his eyes scanned for only one board.

The place had evolved for the better. He casually walked around & entered the semi-open-air complex. There, on the first floor, stood a proud billboard – *Vidya Auto Spares Pvt. Ltd.* Vivaan kept gazing at it as he walked towards it. A small flight of stairs and he was there.

The gate was locked. The wide metal-glass door was shielded by a layer of wrought-iron channel bars. It was a small office that could probably seat 6-8 people. He tried to peep inside. There he got a glimpse of his father's small cabin and the red executive chair on which he had spent countless hours as a child. "Hey! Who is it?" a voice startled him. Vivaan was taken aback and looked to his right. A security guard had spotted him.

"Sir, who do you want to see? The complex is closed," the guard exclaimed. Vivaan took a deep breath. "Don't worry. I am the son of the owner," he said. "Oh! Mr. Anand? How is he, sir?" the Guard asked excitedly.

"...He is fine now..." Vivaan saw a few unopened letters stuck between the iron bars. As he picked them up, he asked the security guard about who else had the keys to his father's office.

"There is one Mr. Pandey. He is the admin of the office," the Guard said. Vivaan nodded. He collected the letters, smiled at the man, and navigated his way out of the complex.

A hundred thoughts occupied his mind. He sank in the driver's seat and started the engine. He looked at the complex building top-down, took a deep breath and sat there, thinking. He then shifted to reverse, and the Jeep began crawling. Vivaan's mind worked on the home front troubles as his body subconsciously operated the vehicle.

On his way back, he stopped at *Uncle Sam's* for some pancakes. He ordered another takeaway of fish-n-chips for Vidya.

***

As he reached home and bolted the garage door, he thought of Mahira. These were the kind of situations where he relied on her guidance, more than anything else. He pulled out his phone, then kept it back. Vivaan was torn between resurrecting his father's drowning business and saving his precious project. He could only completely save one and let the other die. Lost in his thoughts, he entered the house. He then remembered the takeaway from *Uncle Sam's* and rushed back to the garage.

His mom saw him rush out the door. "Vivaan, breakfast?" she asked. Her question went unheard, however.

Vivaan came back with two brown paper bags. Vidya exclaimed - "You went to *Sam's* early in the morning? Huh!" she said as she sniffed her favourite fish-n-chips. Vivaan gave her a sarcastic teasing smile as he handed her the bag.

"Is dad awake?" he asked.

"Ya, I think he is on the terrace," Vidya said as she went to the kitchen to help her mother. Vivaan went up the stairs, two at a time, towards the terrace.

***

Dad was lost in contemplation. Vivaan walked up to him. Rishi felt his presence and smiled.

"How is your Jeep running, son?" Vivaan smiled and said - "Just as I'd left it. And how are you feeling, Dad?"

Rishi removed his spectacles, rubbed its lenses with his *Kurta* and said - "Better." His tone pacified Vivaan. Both leaned against the strong metal railing, absorbing the beautiful morning.

Then Vivaan broke a new discourse. "How many people are working at the office, Dad?"

Rishi looked at him. "Eight, son," he said.

"And how many lenders do we owe?" His dad remained silent. The question disturbed him inside. Vivaan could see the distress on his father's face.

"Dad, there is nothing to worry about. I just need to know." A moment of silence prevailed between the duo, before his dad replied, "Two Private lenders and one bank."

Vivaan thought of telling his dad about the resignation of 5 of his employees, whose letters he had found this morning. He decided not to.

"Okay, what about the inventory? How much cash do we have tied to it?" He asked.

"About 3 million," Rishi replied.

"One last thing I want to know, Dad. How much does the company have in the bank, I mean liquid funds?"

"...A few thousand bucks maybe. The credit cards are overdrawn too," Rishi said as if feeling ashamed of where life had cornered him.

Vivaan patted his father's back. "Dad, it is really fine. It is just business. I will be looking after the office from tomorrow on."

Just then Vivaan's phone rang. It was Mahira.

Vivaan excused himself and responded. "Hey! Good that you called! How are you and how is everything?" he asked.

"Same old, same old," she said. "I'll keep it short, Vivaan. Someone copied all our project files from the lab's drive last night. I saw the recordings in the security footage, it was not clear though."

"Where is Ellie?" he asked.

"I don't know. But she did not come in yesterday... Oh! Do you mean...?"

"Find Ellie, Mahira. Don't tell anyone on the team. Do inform the HOD. Keep me updated," he said.

Chapter 7

Amrita walked up the white, tiled stairs leading to the upper floor. The first brown oakwood door belonged to her son's bedroom.

She placed a tall glass tumbler sealed with a red silk cloth on a small table placed for service right beside the door. She knocked on the door. She then called Vivaan, only to elicit no response from inside the room. She clicked the door anyway. It was open. She collected the tumbler and silently flung the door open. The smell, the sight – they shorted every maternal wire of affection inside her.

The mattress hung out of the bed. The sheet was somewhere under it. The room smelled like the chimney of a tobacco manufacturing unit. A bottomed-down Charlie's 50-Years Old special blend whiskey bottle stood on the shelf right beside Vivaan's bed. He lay there on the bed, belly-down, face dug into the pillow.

Amrita's eyes couldn't bear this sight. She almost dropped the tumbler. Then – Vidya arrived. She stood with a funny meme on her smartphone that she'd wanted to share with her brother. From behind Amrita, she was in awe of what she saw. But not as moved as her mother. She knew his brother was under stress.

Amrita rushed to the bed. She jolted Vivaan out of sleep. "Vivaan," her voice indicated disappointment and worry. Her son woke up with sore eyes and a brain that was reluctant to work for the day. Though it quickly recognized the changing colours on Amrita's face and the big question mark on Vidya's. Then, deeper reality hit him. Vivaan kicked the blanket away and wildly searched for his cellphone.

"Vivaan. What is the matter?" Amrita stood up and Vidya drew closer to them.

"Bad hangover?" Vidya asked.

"Hangover? What is a hangover?" Amrita looked at their faces, puzzled and furious. She frantically looked for the pack of Marlboro on the floor and picked it up. She held it in front of Vivaan's eyes that struggled to find his cellphone.

"You smoke and drink now? Vivaan? Is that it?" Amrita zeroed in on his son. Vidya tried to calm her down, "*Maa*…"

"Don't do that to me, Vidya, don't intervene. I need him to speak," Amrita said. Vivaan found his phone amid the ladies' conversation. Its screen notified 7 Missed calls.

He jumped out of the bed and headed straight out of the room. His disobedience fell upon his mom's head like thunder. She watched him walk away in disbelief - "Now you are going to pretend I am nothing to you?"

Vidya consoled her, "He is… he is obviously occupied with something urgent, *Maa*."

She tailed her brother who had floundered down the stairs. "Brother!" Vidya called him. With a firm momentum, Vivaan kept walking and exited the main door of the house. He was followed by Vidya to the garden which was being bathed with sprinklers. Vivaan took a deep breath and turned to his sister.

"What is the matter?" She asked.

Vivaan quietly pulled one lawn chair and asked Vidya to sit. He then occupied the other one. Vidya lowered her head and stared directly into her brother's eyes. He leaned back, not very comfortable being stared at.

"Hey! You can stop looking at me like that," the annoyed Vivaan said.

Vidya was taken aback. "Okay, okay!" Vivaan looked at the big parabolic window through which her mother peeped at both of them – like paparazzi outside the parliament.

Vivaan leaned forward - "Listen, Vidya! The situation... umm. My personal situation is a little complicated. I need your help." The frown of attention manifested on Vidya's temple. Vivaan told her all about his sabotaged project and their father's deteriorating business.

"All this while, he never told me once," Vidya was hurt that her father had kept a grave secret from her. Vivaan told her that even he wasn't aware of it until a few days ago.

"Vidya, I need a trustworthy person looking after my back. Mom has no idea about all this, and neither will she – I don't want another patient in the house," Vivaan explained.

"Well, what do you need me for?" she asked.

"You are a post-graduate in Business Administration. *Vidya Auto Spares* will now be run by its rightful owner..." he said. Vivaan saw his sister's eyes become bigger. Vidya was about to put forth a ton of questions. But before she could utter her first word, Vivaan said - "And, I'll be guiding you. Mostly remotely. But you'll have my supervision. All I need is a trustworthy person on the shop floor."

Vidya stood up - "You know this is too much, Vivaan. I've never run a business. I am made for the corporate world. I am not sure if I can handle this."

Vivaan got up and pacified her little sister's head with his warm hands. With a pat on her shoulder, he said - "Trust me, you are made for this. I can see you already doing very well. Haha!"

"As if you are a shaman," Vidya said.

The duo began walking indoors. "Hey! Wait," Vivaan halted. "What about the crime scene in my bedroom that mom discovered?"

"Oh! She'll understand," Vidya said as she pulled her big brother inside the house.

Amrita stood there; her gaze still fixed on Vivaan. "Care to explain this now?" she asked curtly, raising the whiskey bottle recovered from his room.

"I was celebrating, *Maa!*" He said and immediately gave his mom a tight hug. She pushed him away - "Celebration? What for? Is this how you celebrate?"

"*Maa*, Vidya has got a new job," he said as the brother-sister duo exchanged smiles.

***

The next morning, the duo rolled their Jeep out of the garage. Only this time, Vidya drove Vivaan sat next to her. Impressed by her prowess in handling the classic machine, a smile emerged on his face – he looked at her as she drove towards the commercial complex.

As the Jeep crawled up to the destination, the two indulged in some serious business talk. Soon, the vehicle stopped at the complex which was now bustling with people. Bright sunlight shut Vidya's eyes, and she rushed inside the complex. Vivaan caught pace with her.

They soon reached their office. "...Remember. Rule 1 – Inventory can make or break your business. Rule 2 - Always remember the figures in the ledger. Rule 3 – Good hiring is worth a fortune," Vivaan reminded Vidya as she entered the premises.

There were only 7 people in the office. Two could be seen inside a glass cabin, collaborating on something. Others were scattered evenly. All of them looked at the duo. Most of them did not recognize them. Then, a senior man with a heavy white beard, round reading spectacles, and almost no hair on his head came forward. His restless black eyes peered from behind the lens. A wide smile then emerged on his face. "Vidya *bete*" he came forward, then looked at Vivaan.

"I'd almost forgotten your face. But here you are, Vivaan," the man said. Vivaan looked at Vidya, then at him. "It is so nice to see you again, Salim uncle."

Age was just a number for Salim Wajid. He welcomed the duo and enquired about Rishi Anand's health. The trio settled in Rishi's cabin. A large brown, well-cushioned chair sat royally in front of the big maroon chestnut desk. The cabin had a big window glass through which the activities of the main office could be seen.

Vivaan led Vidya to the big brown chair - "There, the chair waits for you," he said with a smile. Vidya occupied it.

Salim Wajid obviously had many questions. "Let us talk over a cup of coffee, the three of us," Vivaan proposed. "Sounds like a plan!" Salim smiled and pinged the callbell on the table.

Chapter 8

The shiny silver plates on the dining table were loaded with a succulent, freshly prepared breakfast. Rishi Anand, the man of the house, sat at the head of the table. He meticulously folded a tablecloth into fine squares and placed it right next to his plate. He turned around to glance at the cuckoo clock. He then leaned forward to grab the pet bottle. Amrita rushed in from behind and grabbed the bottle and glass before Rishi could. The man leaned back slowly, sighed,and looked into the eyes of his wife.

The ephemeral moment was vanquished by the tapping of shoes approaching downstairs. Vivaan, dressed in formal clothing – a pair of white trousers and a dark blue shirt. Vidya sported a white kurta with black leggings and a dupatta – and hurriedly sat on the chairs.

"Ah! The kids are here," Amrita said as she occupied a chair right beside her husband. "Grab your plates, you two, and what is the event?" she asked.

"Oh! We are going to the office. Made a few crucial appointments at 10 and 11 today," Vivaan said with a mouthful of a banana.

"And Vidya?"

"I'll be helping him out, his accounting is weak," Vidya said, teasing Vivaan.

Their father almost got the complete picture of whatever the kids were trying to do. His mild smile spoke volumes about his faith in his children. He kept silent.

"Something is always cooking with you kids. Whatever, fuel-up for the day," Amrita said.

The sibling duo had already abandoned their seating. They grabbed a few more fruits and rushed out the door. Vidya threw the bag at Vivaan and snatched the car keys - "I am driving." Their mom looked at her kids' newfound eccentric behaviour, to which Rishi casually replied, "Like both of them are going to school, huh!"

A frown of doubt came on Vidya's face - "Wait! We are not taking that silly Jeep of yours to the office, right?"

Vivaan's authentic clueless face turned to his sister. "Yes, we are. Why?"

"My hair!!" Vidya protested. Vivaan could only gape at her issue. He sighed. She ran back to grab the keys of their small, brown hatchback.

***

Vivaan noticed every movement his sister made to operate the vehicle. The confidence with which she handled the steering wheel, shifting to the right gear at the right speed, cornering and focusing. He experienced an urge to correct her 'lane driving.' He chose to remain silent and let her sister enjoy every bit of the road instead.

"You don't drive enough here?" he asked as he tuned into his favourite FM Channel.

"Sometimes. Not as a routine, though," she replied.

"How well do you know Salim Wajid?" Vivaan asked.

"Know? As in his history?" Vidya asked.

"I mean as a person. Do you think he is a man of ethics?" Vivaan asked.

A short pause later, Vidya said that she had seen him close to their dad since childhood. "There is no reason to think otherwise. But why do you ask?"

Vivaan's eyes narrowed as he put on his thinking cap and looked out the fast-moving scenery. "No reason. Just wanted to tell you not to let personal emotions cloud your judgement in the business. Wajid has been our Accountant for a long time. I want you to keep a close eye on every employee's activities," he said.

"You mean, spy on them?" Vidya asked innocently as she muscled the steering to the left, towards the complex.

Vivaan chuckled. "No, don't spy on them," he said with a wide smile. "Just hold them accountable for what they do. Set goals and motivate them to achieve it," he said, getting out of the car. Vidya's door thudded and Vivaan now assumed the driver's position. He forwarded his empty palm - "Keys please!"

"Where are you going now?" Vidya asked.

"Somebody's got to get a few big clients, remember?" He chuckled again. Vidya smiled at him.

"See ya at lunch. Most probably," Vivaan said as he settled into the car and adjusted the seating to his liking.

***

His eyes peered through the windshield, scanning boards of all the businesses in the area. He drove a few kilometers to reach the city centre. His vision fixated on one of the signboards that read - *S.S. Garages.* With a mellow turn, Vivaan pulled the car over the curb and stepped out. With a cellphone and a black folder in hand, he paced towards the garage.

It was essentially a large warehouse with a tin roof and good ventilation. The place was well lit. There were about a dozen cars on the floor waiting to be fixed. Some of them were being attended to by the mechanics. A strong smell of motor oil and grease welcomed Vivaan. He figured the corner where a small wooden cabin rested. Vivaan trekked through the pile of tools, sporadic welds and questioning eyes of mechanics who thought he was someone wanting to take back his car.

He reached the door. On it was a rusted silver nameplate that read – *Samrat Singh (Owner & Manager).* Vivaan knocked on the door. "Come in," a heavy, trudging voice emerged from inside the cabin. Vivaan stepped into the cabin that lurched under his weight. He closed the door behind him and came across a pot-bellied man with a heavy orange turban on his head. His beard and moustache were impressively thick and peppered with white hair. He lowered his head to see Vivaan clearly over his glasses.

"Yes?" the man asked.

Vivaan smiled. "Hi, I am Vivaan. I am actually here to get my car fixed," he said.

"Oh! What happened? What do you drive?" the man asked. He then suddenly offered him a handshake. With a cunning smile, he apologized - "I am Samrat, by the way!"

Vivaan settled on the chair. "Well, I drive a Willy Jeep," he said. "It stood in my garage for a long time. Now I don't think the engine is producing the torque as it should. I am not just confident enough to drive it on steep climbs," Vivaan continued.

Just then, Samrat spoke- "Hmm... I've seen that with old Willys. I have fixed plenty at the club."

Vivaan gave an impression of being impressed by raising his brows and acknowledging Samrat's claim. "Bravo! When can I bring it here then?"

"Whenever you like. It is your garage," Samrat said with a grand smile.

Vivaan smiled and almost got up to leave. He then settled back in. "Thanks, Samrat *Ji* for promising to save my Willy Jeep, haha! May I know one thing?" Vivaan asked. Samrat nodded.

"Where do you purchase your spare parts from? I mean, I would like to know what will go inside my car!"

Samrat peered through his glasses again, surprised by the man's inquisitiveness. "Uh... We source locally. There are some small manufacturers around," he said.

"Are your customers not bothered about not using branded parts?"

"I've never really had a complaint if that is what you are asking!" Samrat said folding his hands and leaning back in the chair again.

"I thought it'd be better if you used high-quality parts that cost you less in bulk and claim to raise your service charges. You'll be earning a lot more."

***

Samrat and Vivaan walked out of the garage, engrossed in a chit-chat. The staff was surprised to see their boss smiling constantly after a long while. As they reached Vivaan's car, they shook hands. "You are a wonder, young guy! I do hope that your parts are good. I'd like to feed my employees a little better now, haha!" Samrat laughed.

Vivaan fastened his seatbelt and acknowledged the man's gesture. "You are a treat to talk to, Samrat *Ji*. I'll fulfil the purchase order soon. I'll bring my Jeep for the checkup anyway," Vivaan said as he reversed the car.

He decided to call Vidya and share his victory for the day. Just then, Mahira called. Vivaan took her through the story of his first-ever direct sale. Mahira was glad for his win.

"So. Any update on Ellie?"

"That is why I called. Ellie came back today, and she is giving me the cold shoulder," Mahira said.

Vivaan paused to think. "Mahira, extract our design patent. We can't touch Ellie. Find a good lawyer and be ready for any legal action if anything fishy pops up!" Vivaan said.

"I'll do that... Hey, listen..."

"Yeah!"

A moment of silence prevailed.

"Don't you think these moments of silence between us are increasing?" Vivaan said.

"...Never mind, I gotta go. Bye, Vivaan," Mahira said as she hung up the call.

Vivaan intuitively knew what was going on. But he couldn't see the childlike smile on Mahira's face when she hung up his call halfway across the globe.

Chapter 9

Amidst the bustling street, a white 30-foot semi-trailer halted, right in front of *S. S. Garages.* The left cabin door opened and down came Vivaan. He motioned the driver to stand by and took out his cellphone. Before he could dial-in, Samrat came out of the garage. He greeted Vivaan with his favourite catchphrase – *"Oyehoye, kaake!"*Vivaan shook his hand with a grand welcoming smile – "The load is here, Mr. Singh," said Vivaan.

Samraat motioned at one of his employees to come over. A young, black-haired dude wearing blue dungarees came to him. Samrat handed him a paper and asked him to unload the truck inside the garage. The young chap collected a junior mechanic and disappeared behind the trailer.

"While they are at it, would you mind a beer?" Samrat said.

Vivaan chuckled, looked at his watch – "Isn't it too early for a beer? Haha!"

Samrat laughed and patted Vivaan's shoulder. "Okay! You can have tea, my friend!"

***

Inside the cabin, Samrat was busy patting the broken vent of his air-conditioner. He turned to Vivaan with an embarrassing smile, "I've asked these bug**rs countless times to fix this tin box. Can't get the airflow to where you want, haha!" He then made peace with whatever the AC had to offer and sat on his chair. Vivaan stirred his tea and decided to break open dialogue. Before he could, Samrat grabbed his beer can and looked at it with disdain.

"Did that get warm?" Vivaan asked.

Samrat paid no attention to his words and quickly grabbed another chilled beer from the mini cooler that sat stealthily beside his chair. "Ah! Finally," he exclaimed as he popped it open.

"...So, the shocker-bearings you ordered will arrive tomorrow," Vivaan started with his gaze fixated on his tea. Samrat interrupted him - "*Oye, Kake!* Business will carry on. You tell."

Vivaan chuckled. He smiled and took a sip from the teacup. "Well, okay! What would you like to know?" he asked.

Samrat took a large foamy sip from the can and leaned back on his chair to ease his potbelly. His fingers adjusted his blue turban as he said, "I know you are a damn good salesman. Tell me more about yourself, your family and hobbies..."

By the 40-minute mark, Samrat retained only a few facts about Vivaan. The rest were dissolved in the 4 pints of beer that brought out his alcohol-addled humour. Somewhere in the middle of their conversation, Vivaan had heard him say something about a local automobile enthusiasts club. He asked for a beer to keep the conversation going. Samrat was more than glad to have found a beer buddy and offered him a chilled pint.

As Vivaan popped his treat open and Samrat raised his pint to cheers, there was a knock at the door. It opened a foot apart and a head peeked in. It was the same young mechanic in the blue dungarees.

"Done, boss!" he announced. Samrat called him in. The dude came and stood close to the table. Samrat opened his drawer as he spoke highly of his guy to Vivaan: "He is the cheetah around here, you see. He gets things done." The guy smiled.

Samrat then gave him a brand-new wristwatch as a reward. Vivaan liked the man for his generosity.

"What is your name?" Vivaan asked the guy. "*Ji, Karan,*" the guy said in the humblest manner. Vivaan acknowledged him and gave him a nod that reflected respect.

Karan left and Samrat told Vivaan the story of how he'd found him, bloodied and high on the road a few years ago. As Samrat wrote the cheque, the duo shifted rails towards their favourite subject – cars.

Vivaan leaned back and stroked his chin. "So, you were mentioning a motorsports club around here?"

"Yeah! Honestly, I have a life outside my business because of that club. I can live my passion there," Samrat chuckled. Vivaan was eager to know more about it.

Samrat suddenly lunged forward as if an idea had struck him, "Oh! You have a Willys, right?" Vivaan nodded. "Perfect. You bring it to the club tomorrow. I'll introduce you to the cool motorsports family at the *Piston Rings Club.*"

***

Night fell on the city of dreams. Just as the Anand family was settling themselves for dinner, Vivaan arrived. Rishi, Amrita and Vidya looked at his perspiring clothes and noted a very faint, greasy smell. "Have you been repairing cars behind our backs?" Mom remarked and chuckled. "Get a quick bath and join us!"

A trail of a satisfying day manifested on Vivaan's face. He undid his shoes and slid them under the wooden rack. He then walked up to the table and lay 3 envelopes on the dining table with a proud grin. Vidya collected them and saw the stamp on each of them, which indicated a Purchase Order. She gaped, and Rishi took the envelopes from her. "You got 3 POs today?" Vidya asked as if she had just witnessed a miracle. Amrita pointed out Vivaan's smirk.

"I am vying for one more big prospect to ramp up the sales," said Vivaan as he undid his tie. He then told Vidya of his new plan to train their sales reps. "You'll recruit and train foot-soldiers for constant sales," he said. Rishi Anand put on his round spectacles to peruse the letters.

"Terrific! I am almost done with backend automation at the office," Vidya chirped. Vivaan gave her a pat on the back to which she reacted with a loud 'ew'. "Go bathe first." Amrita chuckled and Vivaan hurried upstairs.

Chapter 10

About 20km to the south, right on the outskirts of Mumbai, one can spot a rusty signboard. Going down that road, one would come across a 15-feet wide metalled road that snakes through the dreamy foothills covered with a lush green forest. The old Willys sped down that road. Vivaan absorbed every bend, every climb, and every kilometer of that drive. Samrat sat beside him, navigating them to their destination. He didn't let any of Vivaan's smiles go unnoticed, the ones that screamed of his sheer pleasure of driving.

About 10 kilometers from the rusty signboard, Samrat told Vivaan that the destination was closeby. They could now detect a distant roar of engines and sporadic screeching of tyres. "That is the signature sound of our club, my friend," said Samrat.

The road came to a grand entrance: an arched gate, almost 20-feet high, wearing a marble and metallic crown cup with engravings of engine parts. Vivaan gaped at the décor. "Must've spent a lot on this one," he said.

"Wait until you see what this secret place has for us inside," replied Samrat.

Vivaan raised his brow and turned to ask who this place

belonged to. "Oh, he is an eccentric man. An Indo-Japanese chap in his 30's, Eiji Tanaka."

Vivaan stopped a few 100 feet inside the gate at the unmanned check post. Samrat took out his wallet to fetch a smart card that let them enter the place. "So, what is this guy's deal? I mean, is he a millionaire or something?" asked Vivaan as he set the Jeep in motion once again.

Samrat sighed. "I am not too sure about his backstory. Just know that the guy's dad is an automobile bigshot who travels a lot."

The jeep travelled about a kilometer into the facility to come face to face with the real deal. In front of Vivaan stood a flat ground, a few meters below his ground level. The area probably spread to a few square kilometers and housed a dirt track, a metalled racing circuit, a large dome-shaped structure and a multi-level garage. "That there," Samrat pointed to the dome-building, "is our workshop and customization area."

There were dozens of exotic sports cars, collectable antique vehicles and even superbikes occupying the area. Their engines hummed and tyres exhaled smoke, all amidst an exclusive facility in the middle of a jungle that spread hundreds of kilometers outside the club's periphery. Vivaan removed his sunglasses and shared his surprise of not knowing of such a 'heavenly' place in his hometown until now.

"Well! It is an exclusive club and really not that old. One can only come in here via other members," Samrat said.

"I owe you here, haha!" Vivaan chuckled.

The Jeep crawled to the place of action.

***

Vivaan stopped the car a few hundred feet from the club's workshop. Samrat gazed at three men approaching them. He greeted them with a loud cheer and hugs. He then introduced Vivaan to his band - "*Oyeyaara!* Meet my friends: Manjeet, Kabir and Manav. The three musketeers in our band."

"And Sam is the 4th," Kabir chuckled. His jet-black shiny moustache rose as he smiled. The men decided to show Vivaan around.

"Let us show you the battle arena first," Manjeet proposed as he led the group to a mud and tarmac pit, spread across some 300 odd square meters, surrounded by a concrete wall. The perimeter was occupied by a few dozen people, some women, and children. Right in the middle of the pit, two monster-sized trucks were ready to pull the ropes. As Vivaan, Samrat and the three musketeers approached the concrete wall, the revving of diesel engines went crazy. Vivaan keenly observed every detail, like a child exploring his favourite fantasy tale.

"Whoa! They are breathing fire," someone from the group said as the revving grew louder. From the speakers placed at the perimeter emerged a loud voice: "Let the war begin!" The audience then witnessed an adrenaline-fueled 10-minutes of tug-o-war between two metal beasts until one of them spewed black smoke. The crowd awed, hooted, and howled. Burning tyre rubber left a distinct smell in the air and the mudcloud was to take another quarter of an hour to settle. Vivaan was hooked to the place in an instant. Samrat could see his dazzled face, "Told ya it is a haven."

"It sure is," Vivaan said. The men gathered to move to another attraction a few hundred feet away. "Time for the drift-track!" Manjit said excitedly. Vivaan halted abruptly. "There is a drift-track here?" he asked with a raised brow and a dropped jaw. The men could see the new chap's amazement.

The group reached another levelled ground carpeted with high-grade tarmac and red-white markings. On the perimeter stood a 2-feet tall concrete wall further crowned with a mesh to keep any incidents at bay. From where the group stood, a couple of meters away was the automated entry to the tracks.

Vivaan came close to the mesh, subconsciously pooled his fingers through it and leaned in to see. A white Ford Mustang glided on the snake-shaped track. Its engine shrieked and its exhaust worked hard to suppress the noise of all that power. Its tyres would face in the opposite direction to where it was going, leaving a dreamy smoke trail behind.

It was then, in a split second, that the Mustang driver lost control and rammed into a pile of metal drums and plastic cones.

The group realized what had happened in the first second. In the second, they were rushing to the spot of the accident. Vivaan ran towards the rising smoke. He saw a figure emerge from the smoke, wearing a brand-white racing suit and a helmet with a reflecting visor. The driver walked a few feet, knelt, and got up again. As he removed his helmet to breathe, Vivaan, Samrat and Manjit came to his rescue. Kabir and Manav retrieved a firefighting hose from one of the perimeter poles and rained foam on the white vehicle. Luckily, no fire broke out.

"Mr. Tanaka, are you fine?" Samrat asked the man. He gasped for the air, sighed, and finally took a deep breath. He motioned to Samrat that he was okay. Vivaan carefully observed the man's distinct Japanese facecut. He was amazed by his grasp of English and Hindi when he began speaking to the other guys. "I am sick of the maintenance staff here. I bloody pushed the brake hard, and the car didn't even hiccup," Eiji said, frustrated. He turned towards the car out of which the white smoke still emerged. Eiji walked towards its hood. It was folded upwards in half, the right headlight hung down and the right front tyre was now sitting a few feet away from the vehicle.

Frustrated, Eiji smashed his helmet on the ground. "F**king incompetent people!"

The group exchanged glances to acknowledge the man's awkward behaviour.

Eiji's temper was well-known around the club. He turned to Samrat, ground his teeth, and puffed with suppressed anger. "It will take days for the new parts to arrive. Am I supposed to not drive till then, huh?" he gestured as he uttered in anger.

"Mr. Tanaka," Samrat stepped forward, "It will sound like a pure coincidence, but we have Vivaan here with us." Eiji sighed and came up to Vivaan. He looked him in the eye for a good 10 seconds, then bowed immediately. "Apologies for not introducing myself earlier," Eiji said.

Vivaan bowed back, smiled, and introduced himself.

The six of them began walking towards the track's exit and Eiji flung out a smoke. As he lit it, he asked Vivaan, "So, what does Samrat here mean about you?"

Vivaan, with a stoic yet firm expression, said: "Maybe, he is referring to my spareparts company."

Eiji was happy to know that his Mustang had a chance of an early revival. "I'll pay you double the price for every part and double of what you charge. Can you fix my baby for me?" Eiji asked as he puffed his cigarette and looked Vivaan in the eye.

Vivaan pondered and replied, "How about you pay me the fair price, but also give my company a chance to fulfil your spareparts inventory? No delays there!"

"No delays there?" Eiji questioned.

"Highest quality sports car parts, no inventory delays, and at a fair price," Vivaan replied instantly.

Eiji turned to Samrat and the other guys. He looked at them and threw a chuckle, "Where was this guy earlier you all? He is good." He then turned to Vivaan and told him the monthly parts requirements for the *Piston Rings Club.*

"Are you sure you can supply that number to us consistently?"

Vivaan nodded an excited yes as the group exited the track.

Chapter 11

The office door crackled as Vivaan flung it open. A few pairs of eyes took notice of him as he dashed straight to Vidya's cabin. "Oh! Didn't see you last night, bro!" she said pushing the keyboard aside, "How are you doing?"

Vivaan pulled the chair and made himself comfortable. "Did I tell you about a big fish I've been trying to score?"

Vidya narrowed her eyes and leaned forward. "I am all ears," she said.

"Well, I'll email you the details. There is this big secret motorsport club. We'll be supplying for them!" Vivaan said as he leaned back in his chair. Vidya's face spoke of how glad she felt.

She exclaimed as she got up from her chair and came over to Vivaan. "You are Hercules, bro," she said and gave Vivaan the warmest ever hug. A smile lit up his face.

Vidya got too excited to sit back again. She began pacing to and fro in the small cabin. Vivaan revolved in his chair to face her. She kept looking up, her hands crossed to bind her excitement, and her face radiating the best smile there was.

"I've got so much planned out for this company," she said.

Impressed, Vivaan raised his brows. "I would love to hear that. But... I've got to go meet our new client," he said glancing at his wristwatch.

Vidya gave him a high-five. "You just high-fived! I thought you were uncool," Vivaan chuckled. "I was cool before you were born," Vidya teased her brother with a smirk as he stood up to leave.

He then remembered something and took out a handwritten chit from his pocket. He handed it to his sister. "Here is the address. Get the team to fulfil this order by tomorrow evening," Vivaan said as Vidya perused the piece of paper.

***

"You sure you haven't heard of this place?" Vivaan asked Raunak as he sped the Jeep towards the *Piston Rings* club. Raunak shook his head, lost in the solitude of the road and mellowness of the wind. Vivaan smiled, "Wait till you see it."

The duo entered the club and Vivaan halted his car close to the dome-shaped workshop. It was noon and only a few people could be seen roaming around. Not many cars were there either. Vivaan and Raunak got out of the vehicle. Raunak glanced around, impressed with the sense of freedom that the place had to offer. "Huh! Some club for us mortals!" he said.

Vivaan saw a staff worker mowing grass at the curb nearby. He went over to check where he could find Eiji. The man stopped the mower and it idled with a clunk. Vivaan went closer to repeat his question. The worker, without uttering a word, pointed him to a two-storeyed building that hid well behind the workshop. It was apparently Eiji's private apartment and was so placed to not garner any unnecessary attention from regular members.

Vivaan motioned at Raunak, and they began walking towards the building. As they reached the front facia of the private apartment, Raunak chuckled: "That must've cost a lot," Vivaan looked at him, seemingly occupied with another thought. Raunak scanned the structure from top to bottom – its glass-metal railings, the curtained panoramic windows on each floor, the ample verandah with a stream-wave pool and a terrace seemingly topped with exotic plants. All of it sat behind a shiny wood-metal door and barbed fence.

"It would not seem professional if we arrived at his residence unannounced. What say?" Vivaan looked at his friend. "I don't know how well you know each other, your call!" Raunak shrugged his shoulders. Vivaan sighed, then he turned back, dropping the idea of meeting Eiji. They hardly walked a foot or two when the wood-metal gate clunkedopen and a familiar voice called for Vivaan.

The duo turned back, and Vivaan saw Eiji appear from behind the gate. Glad, Vivaan greeted him and introduced Raunak to Eiji, who invited them in. "I saw you come down from the upper floor. Thought you were gonna ring the bell, but you didn't," Eiji said, lighting a cigarette. He motioned at both the men to follow him to an underground level. Raunak and Vivaan exchanged looks as they followed Eiji through a well-lit flight of stairs. The trio ended up one level below the surface, into a dark hall.

"Where are we?" Vivaan asked and his voice reverberated. Eiji clapped twice and in an instant, the hall was drenched in soothing light. The edges of the place carried orange neon lights, like blood in veins. Resting places like chairs, an eating lounge and a bar glowed under blue light. But the eyes of any person in that place involuntarily fell to the special attractions highlighted with bright white light. Eiji's prized car collection, of five unique vehicles, which was modestly tagged at several million. Vivaan and Raunak were hypnotized for moments.

"This is my solace. My happy place if you'd like, haha," Eiji said with a grin as he walked over to the cocktail bar. "What will you fellas have?" he asked, leaning on the bar. Raunak gladly asked for a beer and roped in Vivaan who was busy staring at a special vehicle. Eiji noticed Vivaan's interest. He popped 2 bottles of beer and poured himself a peg of old *Yamakazi* whiskey.

The gentlemen sat in a lounge that glowed like fire under the lights. The guys cheered and Eiji once again noticed Vivaan trying to peek at one of his cars.

Eiji took a sip and said, "I see the *Skyline 2000GT* has caught your attention, my friend! Excellent choice," he said, raising his glass to honour his newfound friend's interest in his coveted car.

Vivaan leaned forward, now excited to know more about the story behind the car he envied. "I used to have scale models of the *2000GT* as a kid. Haha! These are very rare. You are lucky, Mr. Tanaka," Vivaan said, smiling enviously at the owner.

"Luck is for the poor, my friend," Eiji said. "Our destiny is in our own hands," Eiji lectured. He stood up, swimming in his own thoughts, and went to refill his peg. Vivaan looked at Raunak and they followed Tanaka to give him company. Eiji looked at Raunak, smiling, "You want another beer?" Raunak declined out of modesty. Eiji then looked at Vivaan to tell him that he'd got a good friend. "Good friends don't come easy, Vivaan. You are lucky," Eiji Tanaka said and stood close to his *Skyline* display pod.

One hand in pocket, and the other holding the glass, Eiji stared at the car as if she were his baby. Suddenly, Vivaan noticed a special silver badge on the front-left of the beauty on wheels. He came over to Eiji, "Is that... is that the *Daisuke* badging? An original one?" Vivaan was amazed, and Raunak had no clue what was going on.

Eiji walked up to the white circular platform, a few inches above the ground, that levitated and carried the blood-red restored metal beauty – The *Skyline 2000GT*. With an ephemeral hand, he placed his glass on its bonnet. Vivaan watched him as if he were executing a ritual. Eiji opened the driver's door and occupied the seat, his right leg still on the platform. Click! Twist! The keys rekindled the Japanese engine, and it was as refined as a flowing river, the vibrations could be heard – not felt. The engine growled as if it were a dragon from within a deep cave. The platform rotated and both men locked their gazes. Eiji's foot slowly pumped the throttle. The fiery dragon was now coming out of its cave. At 1000 RPM, it roared, at 3000, it made the death rattle. And... at 6000 RPM it made the death rattle that begged to fly this metal beast as fast as 330 Kmph. The magical thing, however, Vivaan noticed, was Eiji's whiskey peg, which was still as a tombstone in a graveyard.

Even Raunak could spot the extraordinary mechanical miracle that was going on!

Vivaan took a deep breath, smiled to himself, and nodded a little, as if unable to believe that he was seeing something like this: a car's engine designed decades ago to revolutionize performance driving, with practically no vibrations at high horsepower – at all!

Raunak, dazed, left his beer on the bar counter and walked over to the scene. His eyes were fixated on the glass sitting on the hood under which 400 horsepower begged to be unleashed. "How the hell...?" he murmured to himself, then looked at Vivaan who stood there with his arms crossed. Eiji pushed the throttle a little more and the exhaust squirted a blue flame. With a quick click, he turned off the engine and ejected the keys. The guy coolly got out of the car and grabbed his whiskey glass with a killer's pride.

"The original *Daisuke* performance system. You've got good senses, Vivaan," Eiji said.

Vivaan smiled, "Man! I envy you," he said.

"No! No! I am just lucky to be able to touch it and feel it. You must envy the soul who designed this system," Eiji said, gulping the last sip.

"What a genius that guy must have been!" Raunak murmured for all to hear.

Eiji gave a good sinister laugh. "Must have been...? No! That brilliant guy is my father. We owe our legacy to him," he revealed. Vivaan came two steps forward as if unable to believe what he'd just heard. "Your dad? Really? I thought... I tho..." Vivaan tried to come up with a reason for his amazement.

Eiji gazed directly into his eyes, smiled, and then looked at the car. "We were like any other family in Japan. My father used to work for some big guys back then. They trusted him and invested in my dad's design. Overnight, our lives changed."

The monologue went on and Vivaan and Raunak came to know the details of his story. About how his dad knew a talented mechanical engineer and had purchased the design from him to refine it further. Eiji then disclosed his reason to settle in India.

"We ran into the accusations of "Tax Evasion" by a traitor."

"Traitor?" Vivaan asked.

"Yes. The same old man who sold his design to my father. He sabotaged our accounts and ratted us out to the Govt.," Tanaka replied with a grin. "We couldn't let the empire fall. We came to India to save what my father had built with his blood and sweat."

An awkward silence ensued.

Vivaan, hypnotized by the sheer beauty of the system about which he had only read, stepped onto the platform. Eiji smiled and tracked his steps as they reached close to the *2000GT*. "Go ahead! Feel what its skin wants to say. I will let you take it for a spin someday," Tanaka offered.

Vivaan's fingers had already landed on the car's cold metal hood.

Time froze in Vivaan's mind, and his gaze fixated far into the room. He became temporarily deaf. His mind went numb for a split second. It was an unearthly plane – a place inside the mind where time was like a road and the object he was touching was his guiding soul. He could walk back and forth in time. There, in the eternal moment, he saw the 2000GT cruising downhill on a breezy road. He could feel the mellowing sound of the engine, and the friction of tyres on the road. He then saw a small garage. There, across the tool bench, sat a hauntingly beautiful girl. Her black hair shone amidst the light. Her hands fiddled with a pen, and a notebook sat on her lap. She hummed an Indian song. She was unlike any feminine figure Vivaan had seen or imagined. Beside her stood the Skyline. The girl turned her gaze up and looked directly at Vivaan.

The guy was taken aback as if he had touched a live wire. His mind went numb for a second. His heart skipped a beat, and he was lost in the vision he had just had. The girl, the car... the eye contact. He was a little anxious and excited. An unheard of feeling of warmth scaled through his body for the first time in years.

He fell back to his senses in an ephemeral moment, then looked at Eiji with questioning eyes.

Chapter 12

The room was poorly lit, and the moonlight created a partial white backdrop in Vivaan's room. Cool sea-breeze soothed his mind and body. He sat on a chair, recollecting the spectre of the mysterious girl. He stared out the window. His smartphone's LED glowed and he picked it absent-mindedly. A text from Mahira read – *Legal is set. Let me know a good time to call you.* It was followed by a 'Good night' emoji. Vivaan replied, and casually tossed the phone on his bed.

In the shadow of the palm tree, right outside his window, scenes from the morning played back. 'If only I could have seen her lucidly,' he thought. Vivaan intuitively realized that whoever the girl was, she was deeply connected to Eiji's 2000GT. He restlessly positioned his head to find a sweet spot for his neck to rest on but couldn't. 'Maybe Eiji forgot to tell me about her... or maybe the girl has a history and Eiji doesn't know about it.' Vivaan's train of thoughts gave his heart a pounding. 'But, what if Eiji hid about the girl on purpose? What could be that purpose?'

He got cozier in his chair and didn't realize when sleep invaded his thoughts.

***

The next morning, Vivaan picked Samrat up from his garage

to accompany him to the club. It was Eiji's early morning text-invitation that had got Vivaan excited all over again. He finally had an opportunity to see the car in action, and most importantly, this was another opportunity to find out more about that mysterious girl.

The duo reached the drift arena where Eiji Tanaka was already present with his crew. Through the mesh, Vivaan could see the car shining fabulously under the bright morning sun. Two men hustled to fit the white racing suit on Eiji, as he gave a final check to his radio and helmet. He soon noticed Vivaan and Samrat looking on to his show with a handful of other special spectators. He waved to acknowledge the limited crowd.

In another minute, Eiji was fully suited and all set to rule the 5-kilometre-long drifting track. This time, a small fire truck stood by for emergency support.

Eiji closed the door with a sonorous thump and pushed the keys to the ignition. The crowd, standing some 300 feet away, was amazed by the car's roars as the driver pushed the gas. "That guy never fails to show-off, haha!" Samrat commented. Vivaan kept looking at the car as it slowly rolled onto the main track. Eiji's driving performance was being broadcasted by numbers on a huge digital screen placed right across the sidewall from where the crowd stood.

Eiji positioned the car before the finish line and a man stood in front of him with a chequered flag. As soon as he dropped it, Eiji unleashed the hounding beast with smoking tyres. The crowd cheered on.

The Skyline GT touched 160kmph in about 10 seconds. On its first turn, it made a full-body swing with a screeching sound. Its tyres breathed smoke and the car moved like a snake on the grass – only, faster. Eiji pulled some more stunts and the spectators applauded at each of them. Every minute, the digital screen showed an improvement in Eiji's performance numbers. Only a few on the still ground knew that the devilish driver was trying to break his own record on that track.

The car sped by the viewing mesh and the trail wind blew everyone's hair. Vivaan and Samrat took a note of the screen. Eiji had just broken his own speed record on a drift track! Samrat hung to his turban in disbelief, Vivaan gaped at the sheer power and performance of the vehicle. "280 Kmph! Unreal, man," Samrat exclaimed.

The show on the track went on for a few more minutes. With every completed lap, Eiji either broke his personal best or established a new record. Then, during the final lap, Skyline made a crazy move for its special audience. It accelerated to about 200kmph, and Eiji executed a 360-degree manoeuver. When the smoke cleared, the car had imprinted four consecutive, perfect rings on the track.

***

Eiji, Vivaan and Samrat sat under a shack in the open, close to Eiji's home. The car stood in the shade and made the distinctive metallic-tinkling sound of the engine cooling-off.

"That was some show, man!" Samrat praised Eiji for his exceptional performance on the track. "I didn't know you had one of those," he said. Vivaan winked at his friend - "I knew!" and Eiji chuckled.

Noticing the light-heartedness of the moment, Vivaan stood up and walked close to the car. Eiji popped out another beer from the cooler. Vivaan felt the heat dissipating from the hood. "It's gonna take a while to cool, this beast!" Eiji grinned. Vivaan kept walking around the car, acknowledging Eiji's comment with a simple nod.

He finally placed his hand on the car's spoiler fin in the rear. There it was –

It was a sunny day with a clear blue sky. The car stood on the grass, off the main road. It was calm and only chirping birds could be heard. There, under the shade of an old tree sat three human figures. The girl's long, black hair was instantly recognizable. The other two figures appeared older. The girl fiddled with an apple. She then stood up and walked to the car to retrieve something. As she went back, she looked back at the car. Her milky white hands slithered over the Skyline's hood. She smiled to herself. Then, from beneath the tree emerged a voice - "Jasmine!" The girl walked back in an instant. As she left, she once again looked Vivaan right in the eye.

Samrat and Eiji noticed Vivaan's perspiring face. Sweat droplets had moistened his brows and he breathed heavily. "Buddy! You okay?" Samrat asked.

"Yeah! Yeah!" said Vivaan, wiping his forehead clean with a handkerchief.

Vivaan came under the shack. He grabbed his bottle and sat down casually. Eiji's eyes evaluated Vivaan with a stone-cold stare. They weren't however, apprehending the question that Vivaan seemingly threw out of nowhere - "Hey! How long did it take the Hon'ble Mr. Tanaka to build this car's engine?"

Eiji was thrown off guard for a fraction of a second, but he kept a hold of his calm. With a quick breath, he said, "2 years." He then looked at Vivaan as if he had sensed he knew something shouldn't. "Why do you ask?" Eiji asked, sipping his Japanese beer.

"Oh, just something that came to mind," Vivaan dodged Eiji's curiosity.

Tanaka sat there, playing with his suspicion, and replaying old memories in his head.

Chapter 13

The rain-drenched the roads, and it was one of those gloomy afternoons. Sporadic lightning could be heard but not seen. He stands there on the side of the curb, afraid to go home. The only lit lamp post highlighted the green wooden door on the street. All the other windows were drowned in chilling darkness. He is drawn to the light anyway. He walks to the green door with slow and steady steps. His heart is pounding, ready to burst out of his chest. The door opens with a creak and a sense of doom grips him. He is unable to breathe. Yet, his legs keep him walking, as if possessed by a force unseen. There, inside the door, silent figures stand with their backs turned to him. He walks by them – recognizes some, and some are new to him. There, on the floating platform, she lays with her eyes closed.

Vivaan squirms in bed, perspiring, fighting the nightmare.

He walks closer to her. His fingers stroked her silky black hair. He pacifies her ice-cold face. She looks like a beautiful doll made by God himself. Her white frilled dress is as soft as her heart. A heaviness stifles his own heart. He turns back to look at all those faces. They are now turned to him. He doesn't deserve to live. He wishes to undo his deed, but he is helpless.

His jaw clenched, fists tightened, and his legs struggled, as

Vivaan's mind sank deeper within the dream's reality.

He is horrified. He turns back to see his elder sister Arpita once again. She is now sitting, looking at him. A teardrop rolls down her eye. Her gleaming eyes look right through him. She is now fading away. He screams, begs, shouts her name. He runs with all his might to hold her hand once again. He can't move. Arpita soon fades into the darkness. The people are gone. The room is gone. The street and the door are gone. He is falling into a black abysmal pit. He keeps falling and realizes that this is never-ending. He cries for help.

Vivaan struggles to breathe. His agitated limbs knock a few articles off the bed.

His voice turns hoarse as he shouts at the top of his lungs. His soul frantically looks for a familiar sound, smell, face, or voice. The pit pulls him deep. Out of nowhere, a ray of light enters, bouncing around the pit. He stops shouting. He is no longer falling. There is now invisible ground beneath his feet that urges him to chase the magical light ray. He follows it and enters a garden. This garden is unlike anything he has ever seen before. A creek, birds, clear sky, flora, and fauna – this garden is Life. He can still see the pit if he chooses to turn around. He does not. A mellow voice calls his name. This is the sweetest, most nurturing voice there is. He thinks he knows who it is. He cannot trace the origin of the lady calling him. He yearns to be with her.

Vivaan now rested well. His body was no longer under stress. His face looked like a content child sleeping within the protective ring of his mother.

He walks through the garden, following the melody of the lady calling his name. There, under the apple tree, he sees the curvy shadow of a woman. He gets closer. There she sits, singing and stroking a deer. The lady is draped in an orange gown. She realizes the presence of a new soul. Her deer notices him, is startled, and runs away. The lady chuckles.

He is now drunk on her love potion. He gets closer and the lady turns to him. It is Jasmine.

Vivaan's eyes flew wide open. Sleep eluded him in an instant. He sat up, trying to process the distinction between the dream and his reality.

***

His hand fumbled under the pillow to grab the pack of smokes, then picked up the lighter lying on the table. He then marched straight n to the terrace in the dead of the night. A glance at his cellphone revealed the time: 2:57 am. Vivaan opened the heavy metal door stealthily and stepped out in the open.

The cigarette dangled between his lips and the lighter's flame reflected in his eyes. His gaze was fixated on the distant landscape which only revealed its spectre against the dark backdrop of the night. Jasmine's face was deeply engraved in his mind. His mind raced to coalesce the strange events. Eiji's car, a girl named Jasmine, a dream about his late sister and then Jasmine's presence in that dream.

As he blew the smoke out of his nose, his fingers hit the green button on his cellphone to connect with Mahira.

Mahira picked up his call after a few rings. "Hey! Not asleep?" she asked.

"No. You busy?" Vivaan asked.

After a short formal chat, Mahira drove straight to the point, "What happened, Vivaan? Is there something you need from me?"

A moment of silence ensued, then Vivaan broke it. "Do you believe in spirits?" he asked her.

Mahira was obviously not expecting such a question at such

an hour. "Spirits?" she chuckled to almost mock Vivaan. Though the silence on Vivaan's side indicated something serious.

"Are you okay? Tell me what happened!" Mahira sat up on her bed and switched on the night lamp.

Vivaan began strolling on the terrace to narrate the chain of events to her. Mahira listened to everything patiently.

"Look, um... Vivaan, don't take me wrong..." Mahira replied but was soon interjected.

"I knew you wouldn't believe, Mahi. Just wanted to let you know. Not looking for any help here. But I thought someone should know."

Mahira couldn't think of anything that would mend Vivaan's feelings.

"And, no! I don't need to visit a psychiatrist... haha!" Vivaan said before Mahira had even uttered a word.

It was yet another shock to Mahira. "How... how could... how did you know I was going to..."

"Good night, Mahi," Vivaan said with a chuckle as he hung up the call and leaned against the terrace railing to let the cool breeze soothe his senses.

***

The next morning, the black hatchback sped through the smooth bends of the slightly wet road from the early morning rain. Raunak noticed Vivaan contemplating something. "Lost, brother?" he asked with a suppressed chuckle.

Vivaan bit his lower lip before he asked him, "Remember that one time when you poured sugar in Prof. Chakwal's car?"

A smile lit Raunak's face with nostalgia. "Man! I thought I was going to hell, haha!" Raunak laughed.

"Well! I need you for a similar job today," Vivaan said, looking at a confused Raunak who had now raised his brows.

"Wha... What do you...?" Raunak stuttered a bit.

"We need to sabotage Eiji's 2000GT," Vivaan spewed casually as he muscled the steering towards the club. At first, Raunak laughed, but his laugh mellowed as he ascertained the seriousness in Vivaan's proposal. He stared at him for a few seconds, dumbstruck.

"Bro? I have a question for you," Raunak's serious undertone caught Vivaan's attention as he drove the car. "Are you crazy? Have you consulted a psychiatrist?" he asked.

Vivaan raised his brow and looked away from his friend and said, "Tell me, are you in or not? I am doing this with or without you."

"But... but... Why?" Raunak spewed out his frustration.

"It is a secret. The one who helps me gets to know it," Vivaan said. Raunak threw all possible reasons at his friend's face who was as adamant as a bull.

Raunak sighed, looked at the passing trees and contemplated how Vivaan always managed to get his way. "Can you at least tell me how to pull this off?" Raunak asked.

Vivaan smiled and said, "That depends on the situation. Just keep reading my cues." Raunak threw a sarcastic: "Great!" and in the next few minutes, the duo found themselves amidst the growling engines at the club.

"Good luck tryin' to pull that stunt off, Mr. Stuntman," Raunak commented.

"You look like a pretty woman when you roll your eyes at me!" Vivaan chuckled as they both got out of the car.

The scene at the club was like any other weekday. Vivaan pulled out a small opaque plastic container from his pocket and handed it to Raunak. "What is this?" Raunak raised the container to inspect it and Vivaan suppressed his hands to keep a low-profile. "Be cool man. Keep it low!" Vivaan looked around and began whispering to Raunak, "This is Gallium. When the time comes, empty it into the Skyline's tank."

Raunak's eyes widened- "What? How...?" as he ran out of words to say, Vivaan hushed him, and they proceeded to find Eiji. At a distance, Raunak spotted the *Skyline 2000GT* being cleaned by a staff worker. The duo looked out for Eiji who was nowhere to be seen. Anticipating a window of opportunity, they hurried towards the car. Vivaan stroked his hair to pacify himself and Raunak was clearly perspiring with anxiety. "BE COOL!" Vivaan showed him the eye.

The old man wiped the car with a wet sponge as if bathing a baby. He then grabbed a muslin cloth and wiped the car. The speckless appearance of the car was the most important job for him. And he did seem content with a well-executed simple task. His pearly eyes noticed the two men inbound. He squeezed the sponge dry in the bucket kept nearby and stood up. With a blue handkerchief, he wiped his sweating face and the wrinkles on his forehead became clear.

Vivaan hurried towards the old man, "Excuse me! We need your help. He is my friend and I think he has dehydration. Can you please get us some water?"

The old man looked at Raunak and the lines on his forehead became deeper as he processed the seriousness of the situation. He put on his hat and grabbed Raunak's arm gently, "Please sit down, sir! I will get you something to drink in a moment."

As the duo saw him speed-walk towards the workshop, Vivaan opened the car's gate and popped the fuel-lid open. Raunak looked at Vivaan for a final clearance. His eyes evidently asked, "Are you sure?" He then emptied the 10 ounces of Gallium into the Skyline's fuel tank. All this happened within 20 seconds or so. In the 21st second, Raunak sat back on the sidewalk and Vivaan pretended to support him.

***

The next morning, Vivaan stopped by Eiji's apartment after his panic-stricken call. He saw Eiji standing with a few other people around the Skyline whose hood was wide-open. Vivaan quickly parked his jeep and hopped to the scene. "Hey! What happened?" he looked at Eiji who was obviously nervous.

"I don't know," Eiji said, biting his nails under stress. He was visibly angry and Vivaan noticed his body language closely. "It won't start anymore. These guys here are clueless too," he said.

The mechanics were having a hard time diagnosing the problem. One of them lay under the car with a torch in his mouth. The other inspected the engine compartment closely. The third was supervising them.

"Oh!" Vivaan exclaimed and got closer to the car. "When was the last time you had this serviced?" he asked.

"Serviced?" Eiji felt ridiculed. "I spend thousands of dollars every month on its maintenance! Mr. Tanaka will be really upset," he murmured.

Vivaan acknowledged the man's words with a stoic nod.

Just then, the mechanic from under the car exclaimed, "I think I got it!"

The group became keen.

He slid out his creeper and stood up, grinding something shiny between his fingers. Everyone looked closely. "Something has badly corroded the engine. I am afraid it will need rebuilding," the mechanic said.

Eiji denied any possibility that would lead to such a detrimental outcome for his prized possession. He held his forehead and uttered a few words under his breath, "If dad comes to know about this, I am done," and then, he screamed like a beast in agony. Everyone looked at each other's faces to caption the awkwardness of the situation.

Eiji's eyes were red with fury. He came closer to Vivaan and said, "It was the original *Daisuke.* My father built everything because of this machine." Tanaka stifled his anger under his irregular breathing. "Vivaan, you don't know my dad. If his heart breaks, he shows no mercy to the wrong-doer."

"Rebuild? Rebuild it?" Eiji almost broke into tears. "NOBODY can do that," he screamed like a psychopath again, slamming his head on the roof of the car.

"Perhaps I can help," Vivaan came forward. "I've studied the *Daisuke Gen 1* thoroughly," he said. Eiji's tears vaporized in an instant.

Vivaan could see the window of opportunity. "I'll tow it to my home and, maybe...uh..."

"Maybe..."

"It'll take a couple of days. I mean, if you think it's a good idea!"

Eiji looked the man right in the eye. He then bowed and gave Vivaan the keys: "I'll owe you, brother."

Chapter 14

Vivaan pushed the button, and the garage door began to lower slowly. He had meticulously parked the 2000GT beside his jeep and blanketed it with a silver cover. The sun was at its highest in the afternoon and the towing crew had just left. He looked at his watch, it indicated lunchtime. He went inside the house. Nobody was to be seen. Vidya was in the office and was about to come for a half-day. Mom and Dad were in their room taking their afternoon nap. Vivaan pulled open the fridge door. He grabbed all three slices of last night's pizza and went straight into the kitchen.

He chucked the slices into the microwave and then cranked the 2-minute timer. Vivaan crossed his arms and leaned against the cold granite slab. His eyes couldn't help but fall on Arpita's smiling picture hung right across the hall. She looked so beautiful, gentle, and noble. Her eyes held a heavenly sparkle in them as if they twinkled in recognition of the late Arpita's birthday. The microwave beeped, the cheese on the pizza slices melted. A tear rolleddown his cheek as he drowned in memories of the old times.

****

That night, the whole family gathered in the living room to relive Arpita's memories. Rishi, Amrita, Vidya and Vivaan, each shuffled through pictures of the good old days. Vivaan and Vidya sat together, glancing through an old album with a brown cover whose jacket was now a little tattered. Rishi sat on the sofa, watching his family relive the pain of their beloved member. He pretended to attend to some work and got up, only to slowly walk into his bedroom. Amrita saw her husband's agony and did not utter a word. A tear rolled down her cheek, she wiped it away softly and smiled, "Arpita was a beautiful soul. Much more than a mother could ask for," and her throat became clogged with unsaid emotions. Vidya held her mother's hand to pacify her. "You were so little. You used to sleep in Arpita's lap as she hummed you a lullaby..." Amrita sobbed.

Vidya's eyes were now tearful, but she held it together and decided to lighten the atmosphere. She wiped her mother's tears with her *dupatta*. Vidya suddenly chortled and pointed out a hilarious instance, "Remember that one time when Arpita *Di* and Vivaan fought badly. He ran away and we looked for him all day. Arpita found him sleeping on a mango tree branch." Everyone laughed.

As the clock struck past midnight, Vidya took her mom to her bedroom and assisted in her sleep. Vivaan mumbled a good night to them both and began walking to his room. He mumbled a soft good night to Arpita's portrait too, and finally walked away.

***

A loud thunder outside the bedroom window broke Vivaan's trance. He laid on his bed with his head nested over his right arm. The left one fiddled with his cellphone and his eyes kept looking at the ceiling. Against the greyish backdrop, different patterns would emerge on the putty of the ceiling's plaster. Once, when a face resembling Arpita's manifested, Vivaan knew that sleep was off the charts that night.

He turned over and closed his eyes – as if pretending to sleep might actually summon it. A heavy downpour ravished the city, and occasional lightning would enter his room. For a few minutes, Vivaan fell asleep.

It was a hot summer night. Mom and dad were out of town and Vidya was with them. Arpita was to look after her little brother, but he was nowhere to be seen. Arpita grew worried. She fell asleep on the dining table, thinking of calling the neighbours for help if Vivaan didn't show up. The little brother came home late, after a good game of football with his friends. All sweaty and unaware of his carelessness, he walked straight into Arpita. The elder sister was angry. She slapped the little brother.

Vivaan sat up with his eyes wide open. He gasped for air and held his head. A few deep breaths and his reality restored again. He frantically looked for a cigarette to escape from the pain of the past. He was out of luck for a good smoke that night.

Glancing out the window, his option to go out for an escapist drive was gone too. Vivaan walked out of his room and went to the refrigerator for a refreshing beverage. He pulled out a can of orange soda and gulped a chilling sip in the hopes of getting a brainfreeze. It didn't work. Finally, the inner entrance to the garage caught his eye. It was a good place to get his mind off the horrifying guilt. With a clunk, he opened the white wooden door and toggled the switches to his immediate left. The garage lit up and he closed the door behind him.

Vivaan rolled open the main garage door from the inside and was soon greeted by a cold dancing shower and thunder. Cool breeze flooded the garage as Vivaan quietly hopped into the back seat of his jeep. Holding the soda can in one hand, he tried to drown his senses and relax for a while. It was then when a strong gust flew the silver cover on the 2000GT, exposing its boot-mounted spoiler and rear lamps.

Vivaan hopped off the jeep and immediately closed the garage door.

He first slipped the cover back on the metal-lady, then decided to slowly uncover her. At 2 am, he was face to face with the motorized succubus that had been a whole mystery to him.

For a few minutes, Vivaan, with his arms crossed, kept staring at the vehicle with the eye of a critique. 'What are you?' he thought to himself. He walked to the driver's side, drove his hand under the headlamp stock near the steering wheel and pulled a level. The GT's hood popped open.

Within the next few minutes, the rain stopped. Crickets and frogs began making their music, while Vivaan's eyes fixated on the deformed engine block. He pulled out a pair of latex gloves and a small torch to inspect the engine. He held the torch between his teeth and his fingers caressed the cylinder heads, the radiator, and the fuel linings.

There she was – in front of his eyes once again.

It was a beautiful, cosy room with a wooden floor. There was a study table over which an orange lamp burned like the bright morning sun. There was a wall seeded with chequered shelves of engineering books. On the chair, Jasmine sat, a pen dangled between her lips. She wore blue denim shorts and a blue top. Her hair hung down to her waist. She picks up a drafter and rules a few lines on the big white spreadsheet in front of her. The top of the spreadsheet is titled – Daisuke Gen 1 Engine.

She looks outside of her window as if to check on something. Jasmine then leans forward and shuts the window close. A cat walks in, purring, snuggles at her feet and sits beneath the chair. Jasmine hums a song, then looks back - as if perceiving Vivaan's presence.

Vivaan calmly removes his gloves and grabs his soda can. This time, he is pretty sure that he had made eye contact with Jasmine through the realm of time.

"Am gonna uncover some truths tonight. Jasmine, right?" Vivaan chuckles to himself. "Time to travel the realms unknown…"

He gulps down the soda and hops into the 2000GT.

Chapter 15

Eiji raised his *Katana* and leveraged it behind his head, ready to strike. His body went absolutely still, his eyes fixed on the green bamboo bunch hanging from the ceiling, sweat dripping from his forehead and brows. His right foot flew towards the target and in the next second, he swung the katana through the bamboo. The momentum of the sword twisted his body which became still again after the strike. The cleanly cut shoots fell to the ground a fraction of seconds later.

Eiji carefully wiped the water droplets on the blade with a silk cloth and murmured to it, "No blood for you since a long time, huh?" He grinned and shunned the Katana into the silver metal scabbard covered in a red velvet pattern. Then, a distant, familiar sound caught Eiji's attention. He looked out the window, and a smile emerged on his face. He could see the 2000GT dusting the tarmac towards his apartment, its engine intimidating every other presence on the road. Eiji ran downstairs to welcome his treasured vehicle after 6 long days.

As he opened the gate, the car stopped right in front of it. Eiji did not know where to start. He was overwhelmed. He lay his hand on the hood and felt the warmth of the hot powerplant underneath it. He then hurried to greet the saviour of his treasure. Vivaan stepped out of the vehicle.

"There you go! Restored to perfection," Vivaan said, his eyes gleamed with pride as he removed his sunglasses. Eiji was beyond excited. "I can't, I... I can't thank you enough, my friend!" he said and bowed several times to display his gratefulness to the man. However, Vivaan carried a different demeanour that day. His eyes registered every action, every word the man had to say. Eiji noticed this for a fleeting moment.

"Are you fine, pal?" Eiji asked, tapping Vivaan's blazer at the shoulder.

"Of course, I am just glad to hand this beauty to you," Vivaan said with a modest smile.

"Well... I don't know how to thank you enough!" Eiji said, his hands caressing the slightly cold metal of the car.

"Oh! I was lucky to have that beauty in my garage. So, no need for thanks, haha!" Vivaan chortled.

"...no, the Japanese are very particular about treating their friends and enemies. You are cordially invited to a heartfelt dinner with me... Tonight!"

Vivaan tried to back out, but Eiji insisted one more time. He then agreed.

"Sure. Tonight it is. Now, please allow me to leave. I must get to a client on time," Vivaan sought adieu.

Eiji bowed again: "See you, young man! Tonight," and he waved goodbye.

The smile vanished from Vivaan's face as soon as he turned around. He kept walking, lost in the mystery of things he had come to know in the past 6 days. He pulled out a small diary from his blazer's inner pocket. The pages were scribbled with small notes, relations, places, people, arrows, and timelines. At the bottom of a page, he quickly jotted down Eiji's name, labelled it with a questionmark, and walked away.

***

The Dinner

Vivaan parks his car right in front of Eiji's apartment. He looks at the fancy building which hummed soft jazz from within. Vivaan looks at the entrance with apprehension, then pulls out the diary from his breast pocket and shoves it in the glove box. He grabs a ribbon-wrapped bottle of expensive champagne and steps out of the car. The jazz music gets a tad bit louder. He locks the car remotely and walks into Eiji's house.

"A smiling face... put on a smiling face," he murmurs to himself and pings the doorbell on the ground floor. In no time, the door opens and Vivaan is greeted by a gorgeous lady of Japanese origin, dressed like a bunny. For the most part, her costume is revealing, and her smile is incessant.

She invites the man in, "Hello, sir. I am glad to have and serve you this evening." Vivaan clears his throat and walks in. The girl motions at the champagne bottle in Vivaan's hand, with an audible 'May I?' He gives it to her, and she walks away. It seems like a perfectly rehearsed act when another pretty bunny-costumed girl comes to escort Vivaan. Her smile is just as incessant. "This way, sir," she motions at him in the most elegant manner.

The duo now walked towards the increasing sound of jazz. A small flight of stairs and a corridor later, they entered a small banquet hall. Vivaan could hear a few men and women chattering. The girl led him up to Eiji, who was busy taking a shot at the pool table. As soon as he saw Vivaan, he left the strike and greeted him with an excited smile. "There he is – the man of the hour!" Eiji announced. The dozen other guests took notice and a few of them raised a toast to him.

Vivaan was intrigued.

Most of the guests were familiar faces from the club. Some were known aristocrats of Mumbai. Across the banquet, a dedicated crew of pretty women dressed as rabbits did their best to serve the guests. Vivaan sat on a couch as Eiji took a moment to seeoff a few guests. He saw an old man in a black suit, drunk to his gills, lay his hands on the girl that received Vivaan at the door. The sight disgusted him. Soon, another crew girl pulled her away, and a third came to the vile old man's service. Vivaan frowned. Just then, Eiji came back to give him company. Apparently, he had noticed the incident as well as his special friend's displeasure.

"C'mon!" Eiji said as he sat beside Vivaan. "Don't mind them old bastards. And these girls are paid fairly, so don't feel for them either," Eiji said. Vivaan gave Eiji a judgemental look with a stoic expression. "Oh c'mon, man! Let us talk in private. It is getting hot in here, haha," Eiji said, and he spanked a crew girl's posterior as she walked by with a tray of cocktails.

Vivaan stood up with the same stoic expression, took a deep breath and followed Eiji. He took him to a level above the banquet hall, into a more private setting. Eiji also motioned at two crew girls to keep serving them at intervals. He opened a heavy metal door, and cold air rushed out. Eiji clapped twice and the room lit up. "Here, my friend. This is where the Tanaka family's history is preserved," Eiji said.

Vivaan walked in. It was not a very big room, nor very fancy in terms of decor. Though, it held artefacts from Indian, British, Japanese, and American automobile history. On the walls, old paintings, photographs, and portraits hung, each singing their own memoir from the history of automobiles.

Eiji stirred his whiskey and motioned at one of the girls for more ice. Vivaan was already feeling bad about everything he had witnessed in the past hour, especially the girls in the costume. "Family," Eiji spoke out of nowhere. "Family is everything, my friend," he said. "A man without a family is like an aimless star that would never become the true light for others. A man with a family is like the sun."

Vivaan grew curious. He began scanning the portraits on the wall as Eiji narrated the story behind each of them.

"What about your family?" Eiji suddenly turned to him. "Ah... mm... Well..." Vivaan took some time to get back to Eiji's conversation track. "Well, my mother and father worked hard to raise my sister and I..." Vivaan said.

"Sister? You have a sister?" Eiji smiled and asked. Vivaan paused and reassessed the man's curiosity. He looked right into his eyes and said, "Yes. So, as I was saying, we had a peaceful life and hope to be like that." Vivaan then stole his glance at the man.

"Parents are the same, aren't they? Haha," Eiji chortled. "Except... My dad was a little more ambitious than the others," he said, looking at the portrait of a man. Vivaan took notice of it. "Is he your dad?" Eiji looked at him and nodded. Vivaan closely looked at the portrait of a young Japanese man, with a thin moustache, broad shoulders and a medium stature. His eyes were sharp and ice-cold. He held a sword inside a scabbard, draped in red velvet cloth. His chin was held high. White vertical Japanese letters ran on one side of the portrait.

"Wow. Where is Mr. Tanaka now?" Vivaan asked.

Eiji sighed, "He is always on the run, he was a *Yakuza*, haha."

"*Yakuza?*"

"Just kidding! He is a businessman, always travelling. He has big plans for our company, *AkihiroAuto Ltd.*"

"Sure! But... What does that word mean? *Yakuza*?"

Eiji burst into crazy laughter. "Dear. *Yakuza* means *mafia*. Haha," he said. "Of course, back in Japan, my father's friends used to call him *Yakuza* because he once punched a guy who wouldn't pay him back. Haha," Eiji kept laughing.

Vivaan chuckled under pressure.

An hour later, most of the guests were gone and the crew girls had begun cleaning the place. Eiji came out to see off Vivaan.

"I have a feeling you did not like my hospitality?" Eiji said with a serious face. "Haha, no... no it is nothing like that... Actually... umm... I am a little under the weather today," Vivaan said hesitantly.

"Ah! There he is... the tough one. I must then thank you twice. You saved my dad's symbol of pride and success and came to my house when you were unwell. That is... a true friend," Eiji said, with an inebriated candour.

Vivaan unlocked his car. Before he could sit down, Eiji asked him for a handshake. "I always bow to people," he said. "Only chosen ones get to shake hands with me."

Vivaan smiled and shook the man's hand firmly.

She is screaming. Her legs and hands are tied. She is begging for help. The room is poorly lit, and the walls are tiled. It is damp in there. It is terrifying. Jasmine is sobbing.

Vivaan threw Eiji's hand away as if electrocuted. The drunk man couldn't process what happened.

"It is getting late. Goodbye," Vivaan said frantically, settling in the car, revving the engine, and rolling the car towards the exit. His heart was pounding. He was sweating even in the slight cold of the night.

In the rear-view mirror, he saw a displeased Eiji staring at him, fading away into the night.

Chapter 16

Amrita sat beside Rishi in the living room. Her worried eyes moved restlessly from one thing to another. She voiced her troubles to her husband who was busy reading the newspaper.

"Have you talked to Vivaan lately?" Rishi's eyes were stuck deep within worldly events, so he nodded and hummed a yes. Amrita sighed, "Are you listening? It is about Vivaan! Can you please keep the newspaper aside for a second?" Her voice grew louder, and Rishi understood the depth of her worry. He calmly folded the paper, placed it on the glass table in front of him and held Amrita's hand in his. "Tell me... what is worrying you?" he asked.

Amrita's restless gaze fixated on her husband. She wrapped his hand in hers and said, "Have you noticed Vivaan since Arpita's birth anniversary? He is behaving a bit oddly."

Rishi gently pulled his hand away from Amrita, removed his spectacles and took a deep breath. His fingers massaged the bridge of his nose as he blinked twice. He looked at his wife to dive deeper into her concern, "Odd? How?" he asked.

Amrita began listing Vivaan's streak of strange behavioural patterns. "It looks like he has forgotten to shave. It is so unlike him. And, he seems to have lost sense of time... uh... like he is always lost in dreamland or something…" Amrita continued but was interrupted by Rishi- "Lost sense of time? What do you mean by that?"

"I mean… the other day I asked him to come down for breakfast… he did not reply for a while and then suddenly glanced at his watch to realize it was morning…" Amrita explained.

"He must have been working all night. He is busy with his project, remember that *Rappy…* or *Rater* or something! He'll be fine," Rishi pacified his wife by caressing her face.

Amrita grew even more worried and grabbed Rishi's hand firmly, "I know what I am talking about. I am his mother… you are not even…" and she was interrupted by the main door opening. Rishi also turned his head in the same direction.

It was Vivaan. He quietly acknowledged his parents staring at him, and then removed his shoes to mindlessly kick them under the rack. He walked straight with a lost, expressionless face. As Vivaan passed his parents, he waved at them with a barely audible, "Hey" and kept walking without breaking expressions.

Amrita looked at Rishi and called out Vivaan, "*Beta.* some tea?" It was as if Vivaan was deaf to her. He kept walking until he disappeared above the staircase.

Amrita frantically turned to Rishi, "Did you see that? This is what I was talking about. Is he depressed or something… God!" she began to sob. Rishi pacified her again and contemplated his options to figure out what troubled his son.

***

Vivaan was cautious to bolt his bedroom door. He went straight up to the room's window and pulled out a pack of fresh smokes. He was too lost to consciously notice when he had pulled out the lighter from the other pocket. A click, fire, and the cigarette boomed. Vivaan exhaled the cloud of smoke outside the window. He then turned to his left, towards the wall where his bed once rested. It had now been shifted to the opposite side of the room. There, he sat on the chair facing the wall. He crossed his legs and leaned back slightly to straighten his back. Staring at the wall, and what was created upon it, he inhaled every puff to relax his soul.

The wall was divided into two vertical halves. On the top half, names of people, small notes, geographic locations, and casual sketches were pinned. A network of red threads ran from one note of interest to the other. On the bottomhalf of the wall was a linear timeline. Every month of the past 2 decades was plotted on it. There were a few question marks placed arbitrarily by Vivaan about the things he did not know.

As his cigarette vanished, he got up, pinched out a new stickynote and placed it over one of the question marks. Upon it, he wrote Eiji's name and labelled it in bold letters: "SUSPECT."

He took a few steps back to get a complete picture of what he knew and where he was going. That is when his eyes once again fell upon the beautiful sketch of the woman placed in the middle of the mystery-solving wall. He walked up to it and looked at it as if it was the last thing he wanted to see in his life. Vivaan was mesmerized by Jasmine's visions. His fingers slowly crawled up the wall to caress her sketch. His head softly leaned on the wall, and he was drunk on the potion that dripped from Jasmine's mere thought.

Vivaan carried himself out of the zone and casually fell on the bed, lost in thoughts of life, existence, universe and beyond. Just then, someone knocked on the bedroom door. "Brother, come out. We are having some tea downstairs, you are being missed," Vidya said in her meek and sweet tone. Vivaan knew by instinct that she was called by either of his parents from the office to check on him. So, he made a random excuse, too busy to decide if it was a good one, "I am not hungry. I need some sleep."

"...You sure? Is there anything you need?" Vidya asked.

"I am fine Vidya. Just let me be in peace for a while," replied Vivaan before digging his face into the pillow, drenched in the mild odour of tobacco and sweat. Vidya walked away without any further dialogue.

In a matter of minutes, Vivaan fell asleep.

It was a serene suburban town, surrounded by beautiful hillocks. The coastal breeze and waves made pleasant music for the inhabitants. Her laughs, cheers and smiles were synchronized with the beauty of the place. He saw her run through the garden. He followed her but couldn't catch her. Then, a heavy downpour left him alone. She was gone. The town was gone. He felt empty, like a vase that never carried anything; devoid of any inherent meaning. He then walked in the rain, drenched in pain. There was a little hut. He walked inside. There, she sat in front of a glorious machine. Her dreamy eyes looked at him. She smiled, like a fairy blessing a child. He walked closer, drawn to her fruity fragrance of being. He raised his finger to touch the beauty and freeze the moment forever. Thunder struck outside. He looked outside, to find the place dark again. He looked back to pacify her. Jasmine was gone again.

By the time Vivaan broke out of sleep, his pillow was drenched in sweat. Thunder roared outside the window, and he anticipated a heavy downpour that evening. A gloomy dream about Jasmine always left him feeling empty. 'Dreams, eh!' He talked to himself. Within seconds, he found himself sitting on the chair again with a cigarette dangling between his lips. He wanted to dive deeper into Jasmine's life and psyche – as if intimate familiarity would get him closer to her.

'*Hmm...Let's see,*' He murmured to himself as he pulled out his little diary from his trousers. The shamanic mind began painting Jasmine's picture.

'*Bright colours. She likes them, she is always wearing something bright – probably makes her feel like herself. Her smile is a showstopper, a signature of her warm soul. She really likes to be with animals. Cats are her favourite. She is a trained engineer. Being surrounded by engines and design plans is her thing. Her eyes are jet black, a marvellous sight of nature. She lives somewhere in a coastal town in Japan. The town is surrounded by hillocks. Jasmine is a natureperson. She loves to hangout in green, serene spaces... And she is in distress...*'

The pen stopped scribbling on the pad. Vivaan paused, comprehending the last thought: "She is in distress. She needs to be saved," Vivaan murmured to himself. He lay back in frustration, gazing at the ceiling, thinking about Jasmine's whereabouts and health. He then opened a fresh page and started listing his course of action. After evaluating options, from informing the police to some 'coercive' interrogation, Vivaan crossed them all out and threw the pen in frustration.

"I'mma need more than that!" He yelled, frustrated. His attention was drawn to the ticking hand of the wall clock. His nostrils flared and his heart pounded as he clenched his fists. Vivaan's eyes reflected the rage of a panther, ready to strike. But he couldn't see a path to zero-in on Eiji, or rescue Jasmine. He got up, pocketed the notepad in his trouser and lit another smoke.

Through the rising lighterflame and cigarette smoke, Vivaan's eyes locked on Japan on the world map at the far edge of the wall.

***

Vidya came up the staircase with a book in her hand. She glanced downstairs. Registering no presence, she kept walking and passed by

Vivaan's bedroom. As she covered the length of the corridor, her mind began racing. Her gait changed, she placed the book by her hip and turned around, as if under the influence of a melody playing in her mind. With a casual gait, she crossed Vivaan's room again. Her eyes peered at the lock which was open. Another quick glance downstairs and she stealthily stepped into Vivaan's room.

What she saw shook her to the core.

***

Things at the dinner table were unsaid and uncomfortable that night. Amrita and Rishi kept exchanging looks. Vidya stared at her brother with questioning eyes as she ate. Vivaan was too lost to notice what was going around him. He leaned forward, grabbed the casserole, and poured himself a serving of the delectable biryani. Amrita saw this, smiled and said, "Ah! Your love for biryani is not lost after all!" Rishi Shakya raised his brow as her wife spoke to their son.

After ensuring everyone's plate was full, as was Amrita's habit, she made herself comfortable in the chair. She first looked at her husband and then her daughter before confronting her son, "Vivaan! Your Father and I need to talk to you about something."

"What is it?" Vivaan asked, his mouth stuffed with rice. He gulped a sip of water from the glass tumbler, put it back and looked at his parents, perplexed. His fingers stirred the spoon in the plate, mixing rice and curry, his mind entangled between the ethereal portraits of Jasmine and her whereabouts. He loaded another spoonful and shrugged his shoulders, "What?"

Vidya stepped in. The meekness in her tone was gone. Her nostrils flared and she rolled her eyes at Vivaan, "As if you are unaware, right?" She snarled indirectly.

Vivaan's lower lip hung open, his face displayed clueless emotion and he was too tired to pay attention to the people at the dining table. "What is it, guys? What is the matter? Can anyone please bother to elaborate?"

Vidya lost it. The parents exchanged looks, to affirm each other before asking the most uncomfortable questions. Then, simultaneously, Vidya presented a hand-drawn sketch of a girl on the table and Amrita asked, "Are you doing drugs, *beta?*"

For a moment, awkward silence prevailed on the table. The trio saw each other's faces and Vivaan looked at Vidya, flabbergasted. "Really? Really, dear sister?" Vivaan pushed back his chair and stood up. "You went into my room behind my back?" He asked, mad at his little sister for the first time in a decade.

Vidya too pushed her chair back and stood up. She was clearly angrier than her brother. "Yes. I had to. When your elder brother is behaving like a freak all the time, you have to sneak into his room," she spewed anger and her nose became red. Pointing to the trembling piece of paper on the table, she asked, "Who is this girl? And what is that sorcery in your room?"

Vivaan's lips pursed. He left the scene at once. The trio saw him flee the scene, like always. As he rushed up the stairs, his steps halted. He returned to the table, grabbed his plate and left at the same speed.

"Of course, you can run away from family, but not biryani!" Vidya yelled at him. She sat only when her dad asked her to.

***

The morning dew hadn't evaporated by the time Vivaan opened the garage to pull out his jeep. For the past few days, his mind had been racing constantly. The lines on his forehead had become permanent and he was almost numb to his surroundings. Thoughts and dreams about Jasmine had rendered him in an oblivious state.

He slammed a small rucksack into the backseat and ignited the engine. As soon as he glanced at the driver's side mirror, he was startled by a fleeting spectre of Jasmine. As he regained control, he saw Vidya appear in the same mirror, approaching him. Vivaan turned around. He stared blankly at her as she walked in with her nose in the air, and occupied the seat beside him. The uneasy tension between the two lightened instantly.

Vidya looked at her brother- "Do you need a runway to get this thing going?" She threw in her sarcastic icebreaker. Vivaan sighed, took a deep breath, and fired the engine. The jeep then buzzed its way onto the roads of Mumbai, drenched in the freshness of a new morning.

"Sorry for the other day!" Vidya said, without looking at Vivaan. Vivaan did not respond and kept working the vehicle mindlessly on the metalled roads.

Vidya parted her flying hair with a little black clutcher and looked at the brother, "Where are we going?" she asked. Vivaan kept driving. A minute later, he pulled over beneath a gigantic Indian Lilac. He then reached for the glove box and pulled out his pack of smokes. Vidya grabbed his hand with the speed of a cat. Both exchanged an awkward look. Vidya slowly raised her other hand and flipped-open the box of smokes. She pulled out a fresh tobacco slim and candidly got off. For once, Vivaan scratched his head before getting off the jeep. Vidya stood under the shady lilac, absorbing the purity of nature around.

Vivaan lit his cigarette with his old demeanour, then offered the lighter to his sister.

Vidya lit her smoke and took the most relieving puff of it. Vivaan looked at her with critical eyes. "How long have you been smoking?"

"How long have *you* been smoking?" She shot back, then retorted,

"A few times in college. I couldn't think of another thing to bond over with you." Vivaan looked away, exhaling thick clouds of smoke.

Vidya turned towards him, took a step back to lean on the car, and looked at her brother with an 'Obviously, tell me' look. "C'mon, you can tell me. What is up, guy?" She insisted.

"Since when have you become so prying?" Vivaan asked her, puzzled.

The two began to drive their rail on the tracks of disagreements that lead to another fight. Both saw it coming. The lilac stood still in absolute silence for the next minute or two. The cigarettes were almost over. Vivaan squished his bud under his shoe, Vidya threw her burning bud away like a newbie.

As they settled in the car again, Vivaan commented, "Impressive! You can start a quarrel and a FOREST FIRE! Amazing." Both looked at the other, then laughed like crazy.

Vivaan's eyes were watery. Vidya poked his shoulder, "Are you crying, the fire hasn't started yet... Hahaha!" They kept laughing for a good minute.

By the time the jeep returned to the garage, the tension between the siblings had vanished. As the car crawled through the front yard, Vivaan put on his serious demeanour and began, "I know you have a lot of questions. I haven't been myself for the past few days. But, believe me, I am fine..."

Vidya interrupted him, "Let it go! We will talk some other day."

Vivaan insisted. "No... listen. I know mom and dad are worried. I am in some professional and personal rut. I need someone I can count upon, Vidya."

She looked at him, her forehead bearing the same lines of worry they both got from Rishi. "I... uh... I think I need to go to Japan for a few days," Vivaan said. Vidya gaped with a 'Haww' and her brother shooed her. "This is for my project *Raptor*. I will tell that portrait girl's story some other time." He then parked the car and couldn't believe how or even why Vidya was so amazed.

She got off the vehicle and ran straight to her brother and whispered under constrained excitement, "I thought Mahira and you were... like... together."

Vivaan pursed his lips and denied it. Vidya then exclaimed, "On my God! You still love Mahira!" She held her hands above her head in amazement. Vivaan smiled, ignoring her silly thoughts. "Japan. Will you handle it for me?"

"Only if you tell me the portrait girl's story in detail!" Vidya smiled and chuckled as she got into the house. Vivaan followed, once again lost in the arms of oblivion.

Chapter 17

Samrat opened the door to his cabin and switched on his PC. He then turned on the AC before settling on his chair. He picked up the intercom and called in a staff boy. In a few seconds, a young boy walked in and Samrat handed him a paper with a list. "Here," the boy meekly received it. "Give it to your manager as soon as he arrives. We need these auto-parts today," Samrat said. The boy nodded and went away, the door shut slowly behind him.

Samrat looked at his to-do list for the day, closed his eyes and sank back into his chair. He took a deep breath and almost prepared for a quick morning nap. Just then, someone knocked on the door. "Come in!" he said before opening his eyes and sitting up. Vivaan appeared before his blurry vision, and an instant smile crossed Samrat's face. "Vivaan! *Oyeyaar!* What a surprise!" Samrat said as Vivaan closed the door behind him.

Vivaan pulled the chair on Samrat's welcoming cue. "Long time, buddy! How have you been?" Samrat asked, leaning back on the chair. "I've... uh... I've been busy," Vivaan replied.

"Well, I just see your invoices but not you, haha," Samrat chuckled. "In fact, I'd just handed a list of some parts that we need urgently, so let me..." Samrat workedup the intercom. He called the staff boy again. "...Yeah, get me the paper I just gave you," and he hung up the phone.

"Tell me, what brings Mr. Shakya to the old salt mines, haha," Samrat asked, leaning forward on the table, his hands crossed.

"Actually, I won't take up a lot of your time, Samrat *bhai*. I need to know something about Eiji," Vivaan explained. Samrat frowned, spread his hands across the width of the table and raised his brow. "That Jap from the club? What do you want to know about him?"

"How long has he been here? What is his family like?" Vivaan questioned. Samrat looked at Vivaan with a critical eye. Before he could answer, Vivaan gave him an explanation, "I know you are wondering why I am suddenly asking about him. I think that guy is up to some fishy business."

"Fishy how? Isn't he one of your biggest clients too?"

"Yes, he is...but," Vivaan interjected.

"There! This is a mean mean world, *Kake*. Everyone out there is into some fishy business. But it is not our job to poke into their business," Samrat said, sinking back into his chair which crackled under his weight.

Vivaan leaned forward with open arms. "I understand. In fact, I am one of the 'Live and let live' philosophers," Vivaan said. Samrat tapped his fingers on the table in an odd-sounding pattern. "This can be about someone's life and death," Vivaan explained.

"Whose life and death?" Samrat asked.

"Samrat *bhai*, you have to trust me on this one. I will tell you the details as soon as I connect a few dots..."

The staff boy knocked on the door, and Samrat let him in. He ordered him to hand the list to Vivaan with just a gaze. Before he could leave, Samrat asked him to bring two cups of tea.

Samrat sighed, fiddled with the PC's mouse for a while, and thought amidst the silence between the duo. He then began, "I've heard some stories about him. Not sure if they are true. But I have my own suspicions about the guy as well," Samrat said. Vivaan grew attentive, leaned forward a little more before taking out his notepad.

"Some say their family is of fugitives. Some say the Japanese Government is after them. I thought about it long ago. I discarded these as baseless rumours stemming out of xenophobia. Then, one day..." Samrat was interrupted by the slow opening of the door. The staff boy pushed it with his leg and entered the cabin with a fancy tray. He carefully placed the cups before the men and served them salted cashew nuts and biscuits. As he left, Samrat regained track of his narrative.

"I went to the *Piston Rings Club* after a friend of mine told me about it. I thought I might find some high-end used cars to respawn. That is when I first met Eiji. He was screaming at this old man who apparently worked as a car cleaner. When I got there, I saw Eiji furiously screaming at him. It was a minute scratch on an antique car. The old man's beltbuckle was to be blamed. We thought it was a forgettable incident. The old cleaning guy had his head bowed the whole time. One very same evening, the man was crushed to death by one of Eiji's cars."

Vivaan gaped.

"I could tell from the man's smirk that he'd had his revenge. Though the police report said negligent driving and impounded the vehicle. The same friend who introduced me to the club told me that he had seen Eiji drive that vehicle on the track, and intentionally ram it into the old man."

Samrat's narrative bred a stale silence in the room.

They sipped tea from their cups to feel the warmth, if any, at that moment.

***

The Jeep rushed through the curvy road and arrived at the gate of *Piston Rings.* Drizzle and thunder ravished the evening sky. Vivaan came to a halt realizing that the metal gate was closed. He then saw a person hurrying towards the vehicle. In a green raincoat and a black cap, the man came to Vivaan pointing his flashlight at the car. He tallied the car's number, held a radio in one hand and informed Vivaan that the club was temporarily closed.

"Really? Why is that?" Vivaan asked, looking at the securityguard whose face was covered in raindrops that shone like little pearls.

"Mr. Tanaka has asked the club to remain closed until he returns from his business trip," the guard said, his radio echoed in-between as he spoke. Vivaan nodded and reversed the jeep to go back. As he prepared to move forward, he overheard a piece of conversation on the guard's radio as he walked away, "Did you send him back?"

Vivaan kept driving in the rain.

***

It was night by the time Vivaan arrived home. Lost in dreams of Jasmine's beautiful face, he was numb enough to drench in the rain and not mind it. The open jeep didn't mind either. By then, the rain had grown stronger, and it took a roaring thunder to break Vivaan out of his love-bound trance of a woman he had only perceived, not met. He wiped his face, got out of the vehicle, and pushed open the house's gate. He then quickly rolled the car through the driveway and into the garage. Outside, thunder shrieked.

Vivaan removed his shoes and walked into the house as he dripped from head-to-toe onto the marble floor. The lights in the living room were off, but he saw his parent's room light up at the sound of his entrance. He hushed into his room and dried himself with a towel. His eyes fell on the brown blanket which soon wrapped his body. Vivaan fell onto the bed after a long day.

The thunder kept growling, the light remained intimidating, and the heavy downpour showed no mercy. Vivaan's eyes fixated on the play of shadows that the lightning produced on one of the walls. He saw a deer emerge, deer vanish, a monster emerge, grow large and vanish, then a lady. The lady-like shadow caught his attention. He sighed, remembering Jasmine. Vivaan didn't realize when he fell asleep dreaming about her.

It was the same door on the street. He was afraid to walk up to it. He entered it anyway. The crowd of people stood with their backs towards him. He paved his way through them and reached the coffin. He felt darkness settling in, the infinite abyss of pain pulling him. He touched her face. It was cold. He looked back. Everyone was gone. It was lonely. He turned to the coffin again. His sister was now gone. He became frantic and restless. He turned back. There she stood, with her long black hair, an orange crepe dress and eyes like the elixir of life. Jasmine walked up to him and stretched out her hand. His restless was gone. He felt tears in his eyes. Jasmine pulled him closer and covered him with a warm hug. The pit no longer pulled him; the darkness no longer weighed him down. He turned to the empty coffin again. There stood a shadow that slowly emerged from the light. Jasmine's warmth comforted him. From the darkness emerged his sister, in flesh and blood.

She smiled and looked at him. He ran towards her and held her hand. She looked at him with love and forgiveness.

Vivaan woke up slowly. He wiped the drool off his lips. His head was light, as he had never felt like before. The storm was gone. Vivaan pacified his chest to feel his heart and comprehend reality. Tears flooded his eyes as soon he recalled the dream he'd just had.

He stood up and switched on the room's light. He then pulled out a cherry-red marker and began scribbling on the wall, right beside Jasmine's sketch, 'Salvation, Love, Deliverance'.

Taking two steps back, he saw his writing. Vivaan then went near Jasmine's sketch and looked at it with all the love he ever knew. As he looked at her, he texted Raunak, '*1 Week Trip to Japan. Are you in?*'

Chapter 18

Amrita hustled through the kitchen early in the morning. The young maid helped her cook breakfast early in the morning. "He is finally falling back into his work, thank God!" Amrita commented as she wrapped freshly fried flatbread into the foil. "Do you know, he is going to Japan for a week," she continued. The humble maid smiled at her and absorbed all her excitement with absolute silence as her hands chopped veggies on the slab. Amrita glanced at the wall clock and called out to her son. A few moments later, Vivaan came down with a single suitcase. Amrita was too busy packing his meal for the way to the airport to notice.

Vivaan sighed, "Oh! Mom, it is just an hour's drive to the airport." Amrita juggled the utensils, deaf to Vivaan's words.

"Did you keep your cold medicine? And the jackets?" she asked. Vivaan nodded.

"And your shaving kit? Be presentable for the meeting, haha," Amrita chuckled. The maid chuckled too as she emptied the board of veggies into the fryer. Vivaan looked at his watch. He then took out his cell phone and dialled fast.

"God! The network coverage in rains!" Vivaan exclaimed, exasperated.

"Don't rush! They'll be here on time," Amrita said as she packed two Tupper-bowls full of calorific meals. She then put it in a small green bag that could be carried in hand.

"There!" She handed the bag to Vivaan. He then heard a car stop in front of the porch. Vivaan announced, "*Maa*! Raunak and Shivani are here."

Vivaan went to the gate to receive the couple just as Raunak was helping Shivani get out of the car. "Sorry, *bhabhi!* Had to trouble you with travel," Vivaan said with an apologetic smile.

"Ah! No worries. In fact, I am glad. I get to stay with the fun-loving ladies who are not scared of pregnant women," Shivani said in a sweet, meek voice, rolling her eyes at Raunak and chortling. Vivaan was quick to carry Shivani's luggage into the house as the couple followed him. The cab driver immersed himself in a mobile game as the travellers made final runs before leaving.

Soon, Vivaan and Raunak stood by the cab with their luggage. Amrita, Shivani, Vidya and Rishi helped them stuff the bags in the trunk of the yellow sedan. Raunak hugged Shivani and kissed her forehead. Vivaan touched his parents' feet and casually hugged Vidya. The guys then settled in the back seat and wavedoff to their loved ones as the driver fired the engine. The car began rolling and Raunak turned back to look at Shivani. He knew she held back tears. As the cab moved away, Vivaan saw Vidya pacifying Shivani. The driver zoomed towards the airport.

***

Amidst the drowning noise of the wind and the inadequately maintained taxi, Vivaan saw Raunak peeking at his phone. Finally, when he received a text from Shivani, he replied and looked more at ease. Vivaan patted his shoulder and looked away, "Just one week, brother! *Bhabhi* will enjoy my family's company."

"I know. I am just not used to being away from her. Especially in her condition. But I am glad things worked out, haha!" Raunak said. He then continued, "By the way, what exactly is this business of yours in Tokyo?"

Vivaan exhaled, looked away for a second. Then looked at Raunak with a casual smile, "You know that automotive research project I had been working on?" Raunak nodded. "Well, for its sake. Need to meet a few investors and prospects," Vivaan said before looking out the window. The cab driver cut through the early morning traffic at the toll gate. Raunak glanced at his watch and frowned, "If this continues, we're gonna be late!"

Vivaan stealthily grabbed the door handle and fixed his gaze on the bobblehead bear at the centre of the dashboard.

The car is rushing through the highway. To avoid the traffic congestion at the next toll, the driver takes another shorter route from within the city. As he rushes, they encounter an overturned truck. The jam costs them 50 minutes and the duo miss their international flight.

"Vivaan! Vivaan!" Raunak poked his shoulder. Vivaan took a deep breath and looked at his friend, then glanced at his watch.

"What happened? Lost somewhere?" Raunak asked curiously. Vivaan shook his head casually. He then instructed the driver, "You will find similar congestion on the next toll. Keep at it. Do not take any other route."

The driver looked at the GPS navigation on his mobile phone, then looked at Vivaan through the rear-view. "But, sir! There is a bypass road just before that toll. We can make it to the airport earlier if we take that route."

"No! There is a truck accident on that road. You stay the course on the toll road," Vivaan said firmly. A flabbergasted Raunak looked at his friend. "How can you possibly know that if the GPS is not showing it?"

"Mine is showing. What is the big deal? We can't miss the flight," Vivaan reasoned to get them off his back about this insane prediction. The cab rushed on the highway and Vivaan grabbed the door handle once again.

The driver is unloading their luggage in front of the International Terminal. The duo is on time for their flight to Japan.

Raunak noticed his friend who was now smiling. "You are peculiar, you know that?" Raunak bantered. Vivaan's smile turned into a smirk. "What is life without whimsy," Vivaan chuckled.

The cab navigated through the congestion at the toll. After losing 15 minutes, the driver rushed back into the high-speed lane. A green overhanging milestone board read - *Chhatrapati Shivaji Maharaj International Airport [14 Kms].*

In the next ten minutes, the cab arrived at the 'halt and go' station of the international terminal, the one Vivaan had had the premonition about.

As the driver unloaded their luggage, Vivaan decided to give him a hefty tip. "Smoke all you want in the lounge. You won't be getting any for the next 9-10 hours," Raunak chortled as he dragged his suitcase towards the check-in.

***

The Japan Airlines Boeing 777 landed at the Haneda airport, Tokyo City at 7:30 in the evening, Japan standard time. The gates were docked with mobile stairs and the passengers deboarded in an orderly fashion. Vivaan woke Raunak up with a nudge. Startled, Raunak removed his eye mask and sat up. "We there yet?" he looked at Vivaan, who was already standing in the aisle, pulling their bags from the rack.

"C'mon, let us go. The cab driver must be here," Vivaan said, handing a duffle to Raunak and dragging his own through the aisle as the duo exited the aircraft.

Raunak was immersed in the immaculate details and operations of the airport. "Man! No wonder they lead the world's technology!" He commented as they moved towards the immigration office and got their passports stamped. Raunak bowed enthusiastically in front of the immigration officer lady. She smiled at him and bowed in reciprocation. Vivaan pulled out his passport, and as he did, his little investigation notebook fell from his pocket. He was quick to hand over the passport to the lady and pickup his notebook, which Raunak saw. Raunak looked at his friend with piercing eyes - he then smiled at him. "You never struck me as a 'Diary' man. What do you write in there? Love poems? Haha!" he chuckled, trying to ignite a banter.

Vivaan sighed, smiled, and replied, "No. I solve mysteries with it." Raunak looked at his friend's stoic demeanour. He then laughed harder.

In the next couple of minutes, the duo walked out of the Arrivals terminal. As they waited for the hotel cab, Raunak called his wife and walked away as they talked. Vivaan dropped a text at home about their arrival in Tokyo. He stood there, absorbing the fact that Jasmine's vision had landed him this far from home. He then pulled out his notebook again, and looked at all the question marks that needed to be answered. He then kept it inside, and pulled out a cigarette. His eyes fell on a board that warned him otherwise and he postponed his smoking plan. Then, an indigo-coloured cab drove onto the porch. Vivaan saw the hotel's marking on it – *Shinjuku Granbell Hotel*.

The driver came out, held a placard in his hand that said *Welcome, Mr. Vivaan & Mr. Raunak.*

Vivaan motioned to his friend to come over and they stuffed their baggage into the trunk of the slick Japanese sedan.

As they thud the gates of the cab, the driver, an old Japanese man, turned back and looked at both the passengers. He slightly bowed and says, "Ah! *Sodi, misted Biban, eh, misted Donaak. I gotta lade.*" Vivaan smiled and replied to the old man - "No worries, Mister," and gave him a thumbs up. Raunak looked at him with amazement, "Not bad, huh!"

The cab exited the airport premises and the GPS screens in front of the passengers lit up. The night lights came to life and both the travellers were lost in the mesmerising beauty of Tokyo city. Sky-high scrapers, people and places drenched in the zest of colours and life. Raunak wanted to capture all of it on his smartphone. Vivaan's eyes scanned every face through the window, hoping one of them would belong to Jasmine. The car moved through the traffic as organized as the military. The crowd was serene and did not feel like one. To the travellers, the city was welcoming. About 30 minutes later, they arrived in the Shinjuku district of Tokyo.

There, right alongside the city square was a marvellous building with huge glass windows. A giant neon board lit the building's head like a crown - 'グランベルホテルGranbell Hotel.'

Vivaan and Raunak walked inside, where two Japanese hosts awaited them with a welcome drink. The hosts made eyecontact with each of the guests, gave them a warm smile and bowed. "Webcam," they said in unison, as a butler rushed in to help the gentlemen with their bags.

***

The studio suite was well-lit with large windows on the northern and eastern walls. There was a queen bed, a single bed, a couch, and a study table. A large LED TV engulfed the western wall and to the south was the washroom. Two mini-fridges guarded the sides of the beds. Origami tissue papers on the table-top and underneath the night lamps spoke volumes about the thoughtfulness of the hotel. Raunak took in a deep breath, "I love that citrus aroma!" He said, dialling his wife's number.

Vivaan laid his bag and suitcase on one side of the single bed. From there, he could access the study table or indulge in the dreamy view of the city from the 10th floor. Before he could dial on his keypad, Raunak barged in from behind him with the LIVE video chat. Vivaan smiled instantly. He waved to his mom, Vidya and father. Only upon reassuring his family about his recent dinner was Vivaan allowed to go. The duo bid adieu to their families until the next day.

Raunak yawned, stretched his arms, and proposed a beer. Vivaan agreed but after a small meal. "Are you jet-lagged?" Raunak asked with a friendly frown. "3.5 hours' time difference can't give you jetlag, haha!" Vivaan replied with a smirk, removing his shoes and socks, as the open wind subtly called his name. The wind smelled like her, sounded like her. Its warmth was like her, in the dreams. Vivaan smiled. He was closer to her.

He heard the washroom door click, then shut, the shower turned on and Raunak sang. Vivaan dragged the chair, settled on it, placed his legs on the bed and switched on the television. Between the draining sounds of the shower, thoughts of Jasmine, and the exhilarating feeling of the city, he mindlessly surfed through the channels until his phone rang.

"Hey! Mahira! Glad you called... We just checked into the hotel..." Vivaan said, standing up from the chair and peeping out through the window.

"The nightlife looks really alive here, haha," he chortled. Before he could utter another word of excitement, Mahira interrupted him.

"Listen! Listen to me Vivaan. We are screwed... didn't you hear??" she said loudly and frantically.

"Hey! Shhh... Shhh... Hey... What is the matter?" Vivaan's face lost every grain of happiness as he read her distress and pacified her. "Mahira... What happened?"

"They stole it. *Raptor M4's* design has been stolen. Turn on the TV, European News Channel 119."

Vivaan couldn't utter another word. He blankly kept his phone on the table, switched to the European News 119 on the TV. The blonde anchor sat with a special guest on the studio panel – a familiar face. A face he had been wondering about in the past few days. A face he thought was his friend.

Vivaan increased the volume of the television.

The blonde anchor flattered the tycoon and made an announcement on the television - "Let us welcome, Mr. Eiji Tanaka, General Manager of Akihiro Motors, and the designer of the *Shogun Automotive system*."

For the next 10 minutes, Vivaan noticed every nuance of what Eiji spoke. The design, dimensions, performance, and promises were the same as Raptor M4. Akihiro had just swapped the name, and subdued the creators forever.

Vivaan picked the phone again. "Yeah. That is the M4. They stole it."

Mahira frantically asked for their next steps. Vivaan took a deep breath, then instructed her. "Inform the University about this. Also, I am texting a Patent Lawyer's number. Get in touch with him. Release the truth to the public."

"To the public? How?" She asked.

"Use your Social Media. Call a TV news channel. Do whatever it takes. Akihiro can't get away with this," Vivaan responded in a resolute tone, staring out the window.

Before hanging up, he asked Mahira to follow the exact steps, "Expose them, Mahira. Expose them."

The washroom door clicked open and Raunak came out, draped in a thick white robe and a blue towel wrapped around his head. He turned towards the loud television. "Hey look! That is Eiji, right?"

Vivaan settled on the chair again, raised his legs to the bed and popped open a can of beer from the fridge. "You don't wanna eat first?" Raunak asked.

"I think I am full," said Vivaan, sipping the Japanese brewed lager.

Chapter 19

He sat on the black leather couch, holding a soda can in his hand, staring at the large LED screen. Eiji raised the remote and rewound the video. The spark of pride glistened in his eyes. He placed his feet criss-cross on the glass table and sat back. Curtains covered the window, and the only sound in the room came from the video playback. Eiji picked up the intercom and spoke. "2 beers in my room. Ask Leena to bring it," he ordered his staff and hung up the call. He rewound the video again and played it back.

A minute later, someone knocked on the bedroom door. "Come in," he said. The door opened slowly. A young woman entered his bedroom with a tray in her hand with 2 pints of strong beer buried in an icebucket and some fried snacks. Eiji looked at her, smiled. "You know, I came back this morning." The young woman held her eyes to the ground, smiled and bowed. "It is good to have you back, sir!" she replied in a meek voice.

"Sir? Leena, c'mon. Why so formal? Come sit with me," Eiji said, unearthing a chilled pint to offer her. For a second, she almost made eye contact with him, then hesitated. "I don't drink, sir!" her voice turned servile.

"I said... sit with me," Eiji growled, staring at the screen. With a trembling in her legs that was barely visible, Leena slowly walked near to the couch. He looked at her, smiled again. "Ah! C'mon. When I found you in that strip club in Osaka, you were pouring beer all over your body, haha!" Eiji chuckled. In a split second, he grabbed her hand as tight as he could. Leena's heart shrivelled. She froze in her spot. Eiji pulled her down and made her sit beside him. "Here," he handed her the pint. "Start!" he said. Leena whimpered under her breath; her heart raced.

Eiji rewound the video again. He placed his hand over her shoulder and pulled her closer. "See that? That is me. And that is Mr Tanaka. The world is excited about our invention," Eiji said, pointing at the TV screen. "Look, that is me again," he pointed at the screen, his other hand slipped down to her waist. "This calls for a celebration," Eiji said in her ear. Leena could only feel her faint heartbeat in her frozen body. His fingers wandered over her body, undoing every button of her red and white jumpsuit. "You were made in heaven," Eiji's beast of lust spoke. He tried to grab the nape of her neck with his teeth. Leena resisted, trying to move away in a futile attempt.

Just then, Eiji's cell phone rang.

He ignored it, continuing to pounce on Leena's milky-white flesh. In the panic of the moment, Leena picked her cell phone and stopped Eiji. "Master! It's the lawyer," she said, barely breathing. Eiji stopped, snatched the cell phone from her and looked at the caller. He forgot Leena for a moment and picked his phone. "Could you not call me at this hour?" he yelled at the lawyer. Then, the lawyer said something. Eiji went silent, kept the phone aside. "Switch on the satellite TV," he commanded Leena. She quickly fulfilled his whim.

On the channel, breaking news flashed. *'Automotive Giant, Akihiro faces charges under patent law infringement. The Tanaka family is yet to give an answer to the matter. Though, the charges have raised serious questions on the ethics and conduct of Mr. Hiroshi Minato and his son Eiji Tanaka.'* Just then, Vivaan and Mahira's pictures flashed on the TV. *'The plaintiffs, Mahira Sanad and Vivaan Shakya have revealed the original said design of their Raptor M4 system. The court will soon process this case. A big question on Akihiro motors after their industrial monopoly? The polls say so...'*

Leena froze as she saw Eiji's blood boil and the corners of his mouth froth.

In the next second, Eiji threw his cellphone on the screen and smashed it beyond recognition. Panting, Leena ran away.

***

"Bro, are you sure you don't want to be in London right now? Because I think you should be London, helping your team," Raunak said, chomping on his toast and eggs. "She'll handle it. Besides, it is up to the lawyers now," Vivaan said as he sketched a scenic view of a town surrounded by hills and a coastline.

Raunak looked at his friend, worried. "Hiroshi Minato is a big industry name. Are you sure going against him is the right thing?" Raunak asked, wiping ketchup from his fingers with a tissue. Vivaan kept sketching. "Thieves are thieves, big or small." As he embedded the final details in his sketch, he turned to Raunak. "Does Shivani know you eat and drink like a fish?" The duo burst into laughter.

Vivaan finally stood from the study table, holding his sketch in front of him. An attractive wooden home overshadowed the beauty of the sketch in the foreground. "Do you have to qualify for an art competition to get the investors' funds?" Raunak chortled.

"No. We have to find this place," Vivaan said, gazing at the sketch, "Time to explore the exotic land of Japan." He turned to his puzzled friend, smiled, and motioned at him to get ready.

***

Samrat swiftly wrote on a paper with a fountain pen. His fingers simultaneously pushed the buttons to make a ledger entry into the computer. One final hit on the keyboard, one final column on the register, and he folds the register. He gets up to take a peek outside the cabin. On the far edge of the shop, a mechanic is switching off the last light before leaving. Dim orange light lit the shop space through which the cabin's light cut through like a white knife.

Samrat loosely shut the door, tallied his wristwatch for the time, and locked his small almirah and the table drawer. He grabbed a beer can from the mini-fridge and flung his car keys out of the right denim pocket. He almost thought he heard a car stop by at the front gate. Then, Samrat went on a quick trip to the loo. As he came out, his eyes took a few seconds to realize that Eiji was sitting in the cabin on his chair.

Samrat's eyes widened, and he stepped out slowly to greet the man. The bathroom door creaked behind him as it clicked shut. "What a surprise, Mr. Eiji!" Samrat said. Eiji looked at him, smiled and opened the mini-fridge. He grabbed a beer, swapped it with Samrat's and kept the other one back. "Yours was not chilled enough," he said. Samrat took a few steps forward to shut the cabin door. Just as he pushed the door shut, he felt resistance. Samrat peeked outside the door. Two brawny men stood outside. One had his hands folded, the other had it on the door to keep it from closing. Samrat locked eyes with them for a second, then retreated to the chair.

"Oh! They are just my friends," Eiji chuckled, looking around the cabin. "I wonder how one works in such a place?" Eiji laughed.

Samrat barely changed his expression. "What brings you here? Actually, I was about to leave, it is already late," Samrat said, looking at his watch again.

"I know, time, right?" Eiji grinned. "I won't keep you waiting any longer." He then tore a paper from the register kept in front of him and slid it over to Samrat. "Here. Just give me Vivaan's address. Can't seem to get in touch with him," Eiji said. Samrat's sixth sense urged him to not listen to the man.

"I don't know where he lives. He never told me," Samrat said.

Then, Eiji stood up, stared directly into Samrat's soul as his nostrils flared. "You brought him to the club. You don't know where he lives?"

Samrat paused, looked into the man's eyes, and said, "We never talked about it. Never occurred to us. All we talk about is business. But, why do you want to know where he lives?"

The door opened and the two brawny men entered the cabin. With too many people, the place soon became crowded. Each man stood on either side of Samrat's chair. Samrat tightened his grip on the arm of the chair. Eiji stood up, leaned forward and held a small knife against Samrat's neck as he leaned back for the lack of resistance. "I know you are the little sh*t that goes behind my back telling people about that old car cleaner," Eiji spewed in rage. The blade grew intense on Samrat's jugular. "You know what really happened to him?" Eiji asked. His voice then drowned out in his own sinister laugh.

Samrat froze in his seat. His peripheral vision revealed a holster protruding from the belt of the man standing to his right. He saw Eiji quit laughing and sink back into the chair. He picked the golden-blue fountain pen and fiddled with it as he reflected on his own act and talked to Samrat. "You know, that old man lived," Eiji said. Samrat frowned with surprise. Eiji looked at him with a sinister smile and leaned forward on the table, placing the pen in its original position. "I cut him later that week when he healed," Eiji said as his cold, dead stare cut through Samrat.

"That friend of yours has created a lot of trouble. Tell me where he is!" Eiji asked. Samrat felt the muzzle of a pistol against his right ear and a big cold blade shining to his left. His legs were warm as his fight-or-flight instinct kicked in. Then the warmth went away. "He... he... never told me where he lived," Samrat said.

Silence ensued for the next few seconds.

Then Eiji stood up and walked to the door. He opened it partially and without looking at Samrat, asked him, "Is that your final answer?" The muzzle of the gun now pointed at his head.

Samrat remained silent, then said, "I know his company address."

***

Vivaan drove a small Suzuki 4x4 with Raunak capturing photos at every possible instance. He pulled the car into the parking of the train station while Raunak was fixated on the Japanese bar nearby. He got out of the car, clicked a picture of the bar, and sent it to Shivani with the caption, *Some Japanese brew for the soul* followed by laughing emojis. Then, he saw Vivaan walk the other way.

"Hey! Bro! The bar is this way," Raunak shouted. Vivaan turned around and said, "I know. But we have a train to catch." The duo then hopped and checked into the *Shinkansen* High-speed Rail network. As they reached the platform, Raunak gaped at the formidable design of an arriving train. "Whoa! Is that... is that the 'Bullet train'?" He asked, trying to bottleup his amazement.

Vivaan smiled, "Indeed. Isn't it marvellous?"

About four minutes later, their train arrived. Vivaan stood up from the seat, "Our ride to Sendai is here." Puzzled, Raunak looked at him - "Sendai?"

"Yes! Looked like a city worth exploring to me," Vivaan replied as the duo got ready to board the train. Raunak, clueless, smiled and agreed. "Okay! Sounds like a plan. How far is it anyway?"

"Uhh... Umm... About 400 Kilometers," Vivaan said. Puzzled, Raunak looked at him again. The doors of the Shinkansen train opened with a hiss as the hydraulics slowly pushed the doors ajar. The men entered the cooled coach. Vivaan entered the code for the online tickets bought last night and he got the seat numbers. Raunak was amazed at the sight of a vending machine placed inside the coach. Amidst the crowd saturated in unbelievable silence, the duo walked up to their seats and settled.

Having explored fascinating sights, foods, and colours of another culture, Raunak fell asleep fast as his excitement wore off. The train passed through cities, suburbs, riversides, and tunnels. The sweet click and clack of the rails were soothing to hear. Moreover, the train was unbelievably smooth for something that heavy moving at 300kmph. Vivaan praised the engineering under his breath and took out his sketch. He scribbled some final details with his pencil. Then, his eyes fixed outside the window.

The mountains were low, dividing the coast from the town. The sea was stable, and the green cover was partial. A large statue of the Buddha sat amidst a section around which some houses were erected. Vivaan was a little annoyed by the darkness that settled in as the train passed through yet another tunnel. As the coach emerged from the other side, the moment froze for Vivaan forever. Hillocks, houses, gardens, and the landscape was the same as Vivaan's sketch. As the train rushed to a stop at the Sendai station, Vivaan excitedly peeped out the window to spot the special wooden house. He stole a glance at it, then the curtain on the scene fell. Skyscrapers covered the landscape and Vivaan jolted Raunak out of his sleep.

Chapter 20

"So, this is the town of Sendai!" Raunak looked around the street as he walked down the road with Vivaan. The coastal breeze caressed their faces. "Just like Mumbai, huh! Where are we going exactly?" he asked. Vivaan glanced at his wristwatch and slowed down near a board that read 'Cat Cafe Asakusa.' He put his hands in the pockets and stood in front of the board, then looked at Raunak, "How 'bout some lunch? I hope you like cats!"

Raunak's eyes widened, the frown of confusion manifested on his face again as he reluctantly followed his friend into the cafe. "Brother, cats? They eat cats here? Is that even something to eat?" Raunak began to lose it. He looked as disgusted as a toddler at the sight of broccoli. "How can anyone eat cats?" he nagged until Vivaan chuckled and patted his shoulder, "You *play* with the cats. Nobody eats them here!" Vivaan said as he laughed. Then his laughter amplified until the duo were escorted by a waitress to their table. They occupied a booth along the glass window through which the street was visible.

Sitting across to each other, Raunak counted every cat that walked there. The restaurant was half-occupied with people who liked feline company. "If this were in India, it would be named 'Coffee with Cats,' haha!" Raunak lightly banged the table to validate his humour. Vivaan looked at him with a smile. Then he sat straight in the chair, placed the sprinklers and the ketchup bottle aside and said, "You have lunch. I have to meet someone here, in the commercial area. I will catch you in an hour or two here."

"I can come with you if…" Raunak said, but Vivaan stopped him.

"Oh, don't bother. You'll get bored. I'll be quick," he said. Then a white cat paved her way from between their legs, rubbing her fur on all the legs under the table. Vivaan picked her up gently and placed her in Raunak's lap - "Now you have company too," he chuckled as he stood up to walk out. Raunak instantly engaged with the cat whose red collar read *Martha.* He grabbed her paw gently and waved it at Vivaan as he whispered into the cat's ear, "Say *Good Luck*, human!"

***

Vivaan got out of the city bus that stopped at the *Fruit Garden* or 'Kaju-en' bus station. From there, he had a complete view of the coastline, the crown of hillocks, and the streets lined with houses. Before he embarked on a 2-kilometre walk, he took out and unfolded the sketch from his pocket for a quick glance at Jasmine's house. As the bus grunted away, he crossed the road and began walking down the hill towards the coastline.

***

As Vivaan landed on the street, the sound of the sea grew louder. One side of the road was lined with houses and gardens between them. The other was lined with trees and the coastline. It was a peaceful section of the town. Vivaan continued walking, trying to lock in the perspective of his sketch. A few hundred feet to the point where foothills began, he came across the porch of a two-storeyed wooden house.

The front porch was blanketed with overgrown weeds. A metal mesh secured the house's perimeter, and it was now home to a lot of crawlers and creepers. A swarm of cicadas hummed from within the bushes, making music about time past. Vivaan's mind drifted in and out of visions of Jasmine and the stark reality that stood in front of him. With heavy steps, he walked in front of the main gate, a broken wooden frame with a rusted plate hanging from it. Vivaan undid the mud on the plate. The name *Kumar's* appeared in bold black letters. He peeked inside the premises. A long corridor went through the length of the entire house. There was a dry pond in what used-to-be a garden.

Vivaan's eyes went from the pond to the upper floor. He saw an intact glass window placed on the wooden frame. He remembered his vision of Jasmine working in her room, glancing out of that window. Vivaan didn't even realize he had pushed the creaky old gate open. As his fingers lifted from the gate's frame, a sharp burst of pain went through his head, then his spine. Vivaan was blinded for a moment. Through the spasmodic pain, he saw thousands of visions from the house's past within a fraction of a second.

Vivaan slouched forward into the porch, then fell on his knees, holding his head to keep it from exploding.

Jasmine's 14th birthday cake, her parents getting her a new cat, when she fell from the stairs and bruised her elbows, the hurricane warning when she wouldn't leave her father, her sadness when her cat died, her happiness when she got accepted into the engineering university, her first working model of a new type of suspension, her worry and restlessness when her dad suffered a stroke, the little berries she planted into the garden bed, the day she turned twenty-two, the day she graduated from college, and the day she attended someone's funeral...

The humming of the cicadas grew louder, and his eyes became foggy. Thousands of memories from another reality gushed through his mind. A minute passed by and Vivaan began breathing frantically.

He panted until he finally steadied himself. He immediately took out his little notebook and uncapped the pen in a hurry. He jotted down, 'Avoid vision overload.' He capped the pen as he stood back up.

Vivaan took a deep breath. Then with a casual, light foot, he walked to the entrance of the house which was in the middle of the long side corridor. A sea breeze blew the wild plants all around. Vivaan could smell the strong earthy and musky smell of algae blooming over the walls. He slowly slid the rolling wooden door with his elbow to the right. The door rattled and undid itself. A gush of stale air rushed out the house. Vivaan took out a handkerchief, placed it over his nose and walked in.

Through the daylight that entered through the three large glass windows on the lower floor, he could see the old living room. Two small couches, a Japanese-style dining table with three large cushions on each side, a fireplace mantle adjacent to the windows and a bookshelf. At the end of the living room was another space beside which stood a staircase. As he went to explore the upper floor, his eyes fell upon an old, dusted portrait with broken glass placed over the mantle. Caught-up in the frenzy of the moment, he grabbed the portrait, seeing Jasmine in reality for the first time.

She wore an orange skirt, a dark blue top, and sat with her head on her father's shoulder. Her mother stood behind them, smiling. Jasmine had an uncanny resemblance to her mother – the eyes, the cheekbones, the lips, and the smile.

Jasmine is excited about the family portrait. Her father is intermittently checking his watch. Then she playfully takes his watch away, asking him not to go to work that day. Her mother keeps asking her daughter not to trouble her father. But her father keeps his daughter's heart. Then the photographer asks them to be seated to capture the frame.

Vivaan comes out of the trance, closes his eyes, takes a deep breath, and climbs up the stairs. The staircase was dark, with light only at the end. Vivaan switches to the flashlight on his mobile. With one hand holding the handkerchief over his nose and the other showing him the way with a cellphone, he reaches the upper deck. To his right lies the entrance to Jasmine's room. To his left is another closed space and a staircase that probably leads to the terrace.

By now, Vivaan was mesmerized by a strange sensation. The closer he went to Jasmine's room, the more he felt like he was being followed. On several occasions, Vivaan turned back with his cellphone flash only to see nothing. Once he entered her room, he closed the door behind him. Jasmine's room was full of daylight. The furniture was placed exactly where he had seen in his visions. Her table, her chair, the place where her cat sat.

Vivaan took a step back, trying to absorb reality, and leaned against the door only to slide down and sit blankly. A few tears rolled down his eyes. He was overwhelmed by everything.

"This doesn't make sense!" he mumbled under his breath. He pacified himself by stroking his shabby hair. "Where is everybody? Where are you?" he asked, frustrated, looking up as if talking to Jasmine. "You said you'd meet me here..." and he sobbed silently. "What time is it? When did you live here? Where are you now?" Vivaan clutched his hair tightly. He then wiped his face with the handkerchief, threw it aside and stood up.

He exhaled excitedly. "Okay! Let's do this. I will find you soon," he said to himself.

He carefully examined the objects and artefacts kept inside. Most of it was covered in dust and mould. Vivaan sifted through many objects. He looked out the window through which the small garden pond was visible. He placed the chair exactly where he had seen Jasmine keep it. He sat on it and thought. Then it occurred to him, "You...you... used to write a diary. Hah!" Vivaan then sifted a little more, finally unearthing the diary from one of the table drawers.

Vivaan remembered the lesson he'd learned a while back, located his handkerchief again and picked up the diary to avoid touching it directly. The hardcover notebook was jacketed with maroon velvet, eating dust for years. The first page read *My Diary* in calligraphy. Jasmine's signature sat on the bottom right corner of the page. Vivaan shuffled through the pages to check the last entry, which rendered him dumbstruck. The last entry in the diary was made 18 years ago in May 1998.

Vivaan helplessly fell into the chair. "That was... was..." he couldn't utter the words himself because he refused to believe them. "Eighteen years ago..." he mumbled to himself. Deciphering the truth took a toll on his willpower. Vivaan placed his head on his arms on the table and closed his eyes.

***

The setting sun's rays hit Vivaan's face and broke his sleep. He woke from a dream about Jasmine, disconnected from reality for a while. He frantically looked at his watch that showed 5:30pm. Then he checked his cellphone which showed no missed calls. "I better rush," he said to himself. Vivaan quickly rushed through the last entries of the diary to salvage any clue about her present whereabouts.

"Let's see... Stressful day log, hmmm... Police complaint, huh?" Vivaan came across a second last entry. He found Jasmine mentioning 'threat' and a 'Yakuza' figure threatening to take something away from her. Jasmine had filed a complaint against someone known as the *'Shark of Kabukicho.'* He then shuffled the pages with the help of his handkerchief to look for the entry titles. "Hmm... You were lonely at some point huh?" Vivaan pretended to talk to her. "New engine design... aha!" Vivaan came across an entry that said 'Fun run on the 2000 GT.' He quickly scanned for keywords. "You designed the *Daisuke* powertrain, then... you had someone threaten you... I think Eiji. He would have been too young to trouble you back then... Shark of Kabukicho..." Vivaan's mind ran in all the directions at once. It was only interrupted when he saw somebody enter the house through the porch gate.

Vivaan hid Jasmine's diary in his denim, collected his cellphone and walked down the stairs without making a noise. He couldn't see the intruder's face. Vivaan grabbed a broken stick kept on the stairs just in case. Then, he froze in the dark of the stairs, waiting for the intruder to arrive inside.

The wooden door rolled and rattled again. A feeble, old man entered the premises. He hobbled as he walked. He first came in, looked through the living room windows, then started coming near the stairs. Vivaan did not see him as a threat and slowly appeared from within the dark. The old man got startled and fell back. Vivaan could see the terror on the guy's face. He quickly rushed to help him. "No! No!" the old man begged for his life. Then Vivaan noticed the stick in his own hand and dropped it.

"Hey! Hey!" Vivaan tried to calm the man down. "I am a friend. Friend! Friend!" he repeated. The feeble old man came back to his senses. Vivaan lifting his arms and helped him stand back.

The old man continued to look into Vivaan's eyes. He pointed at him, as if he had seen a spectre after being haunted by one in his dreams. His hands shook. Vivaan noticed that he was Indian.

"Who are you?" Vivaan asked.

"Who are you?" the man whispered as his eyes widened.

"I am Vivaan... from India," he replied.

"Where is she? Is she back yet?" the old man whispered and asked him instead.

"Who 'she'? And who are you?" Vivaan asked.

"I am Samartha. Mr. Kumar's property manager," the man replied, scanning Vivaan with suspicion.

"What are you doing here?" Samartha asked. Vivaan didn't have an answer.

"What are *you* doing here?" Vivaan countered.

"I am the manager of this property. I saw the gate open. I thought somebody broke in," the man replied with a heavy groan.

***

They walked out of the house and Vivaan asked if he could light a cigarette there. The old man didn't mind. Vivaan walked by the hobbling man, listening to his story. "I had known the girl since she was seven. Such a sweet angel," Samartha's voice cracked. "Jasmine's early life was good. Tragedy struck her when her parents passed away," the old man sobbed.

Shocked, Vivaan turned to him. "What?" he sounded puzzled. "Jasmine's parents died? How?" he asked.

"Well," Samartha bounced back from his nostalgia. "There was a car accident. It was Jasmine's twenty-second birthday. Mr. and Mrs. Kumar were rushing back from the office. Their car fell downthe cliff and was never recovered from the ocean-bed," Samartha sobbed. Vivaan was heartbroken by the story. He smoked, looked at the house once again before leaving. He then immediately turned to the old man. "Where is Jasmine now?" he asked, his eyes glistening with hope.

The old man looked at Jasmine's old room window, then turned to Vivaan. "A year after the passing of her parents, she vanished... In 1998, I guess. Nobody has seen her since," Samartha said. "I come here every week to see if she is back. I want to see how she has grown up to be. She looked just like Mrs. Kumar..." the man continued.

Vivaan crossed his arms and listened to the old man. Then he asked, "Was anyone troubling her? A 'Yakuza,' perhaps? Someone after her business now that she was the only heir?"

The old man stood silent. The sun had almost set. The cicadas were long gone. The orange sky melded with the rising night sky. Samartha hobbled and walked out of the broken gate. Vivaan smoked and tracked his every step. The man sat on his moped and gave it a jolt with his leg to kickstart it. Vivaan came to him again. "If you know something, tell me," he said, looking in Samartha's eye.

"I would guess the 'Shark of Kabukicho' had something to do with this," Samartha replied, as he raced his moped towards the far end of the road.

***

The night Shinkansen train to Tokyo had arrived. Raunak and Vivaan settled in again. Raunak noticed his worn-off friend. He handed him a Tupper of fried fish. "Man! This has to be the best fried fish here," Raunak said. Vivaan smiled, accepted the Tupper and looked out the window. The train picked up speed faster than the wind. Raunak pulled out his earphones and decided to sleep through the ride.

Vivaan pulled out his cellphone and searched for 'Shark of Kabukicho.' Old articles and news stories from the '90s flooded his search results. He translated them from Japanese to English. Following on a few news stories of extortion, murder, and kidnapping, Vivaan felt butterflies in his stomach. He rested his head against the windowpane as the coach's lights dimmed. Vivaan held himself together with all his might, trying not to break down. "What happened to you Jasmine?" he asked himself.

The Japanese citylights took his mind off Jasmine until he fell asleep.

Chapter 21

Welcome to Kabukicho

Before sunset the next day, Vivaan got ready. He wore a black jacket, light blue jeans, and a red shirt. He wore heavy boots to tread strongly into the unknown. His online research about the *Kabukicho* area revealed it to be the adult entertainment centre of Tokyo. Vivaan had already made his mind up about shady corners fraught with dangerous cartel members who happened to run such places around the world. Just different names, different businesses, and different methods.

Raunak was asleep. He had plans to explore the local area when he woke up. Vivaan left him a text message and came out of the hotel. He had no clue where to begin. Only a reference to a man known as the 'Shark' in the '90s. Vivaan stopped a cab and told him his destination. About thirty minutes later, he arrived at his destination.

Vivaan saw a big red and blue neon board above the infamous street. From where he stood, he could see an endless row of nightclubs, strip clubs, restaurants, and people. Kabukicho was like any other part of Tokyo, only it ran a collection of successful 'Adult entertainment' businesses established here years ago. Vivaan walked through the streets looking for a hint. Men and women moved freely. A few restaurant owners stood in front of their boards, smoking cigarettes. Vivaan even saw a big blue digital screen on one of the buildings that advertised a 'sex robot' for those who fancied such a thing.

Vivaan walked over to a vendor selling meat dumplings. He grabbed a chair, sat, and waited there. The vendor, probably in his 40's without any facial hair, changed his chef cap, wore new gloves and turned to Vivaan. He smiled, bowed, and asked him - 餃子はいかがですか？ (Would you like some dumplings?).

"Umm…" Vivaan bowed back and said, "No Japanese… English? You speak English, sir?"

"Ahhh… ingliss… Ahhh" The vendor seemed to be familiar with the language. "I'll try the steamed fish dumplings," Vivaan said pointing to an item on the menu that hung in front of the small wooden stall.

As the utensils huffed out steam, Vivaan looked around the street. On the other side of the street, he saw two girls wearing tight black latex suits, trying to woo him. One of them blew a kiss at him, while the other encouraged him to come over, motioning at him with a finger. Vivaan ignored them. The man served him five piping hot dumplings on a porcelain plate. He topped them with cheese-garlic dip and mint leaves. Vivaan had no interest in the food. Though he ate one and began to chit-chat with the vendor.

Then, Vivaan translated 'Shark of Kabukicho' into Japanese with his Smartphone - 歌舞伎町のサメ. As soon as he showed it to the vendor, he flipped, incessantly shaking his head in a big 'no.' Vivaan insisted. The guy drove him out of his stall. Disappointed, Vivaan paid the guy, grabbed another dumpling, and left. The two girls from the other side of the street giggled to which Vivaan paid no attention. He kept walking. The girls were quick to follow him.

Vivaan passed by a bar where a man in a black hoodie tried to hawk him inside. "C'mon, fun, lots of girls and booze. C'mon!" the man kept hooking him. Vivaan ignored it. Then, he crossed an alleyway lined with big dumpsters where the restaurants would discard all their waste. The girls in the latex crossed the street and confronted Vivaan. One of the girls was a blonde westerner, the other was a Japanese. "Where ya sailing, skipper?" the blonde spoke flirtatiously. She stroked Vivaan's jacket. The Japanese girl flaunted her curves and began, "We kiss you, you give us money, okay?"

Vivaan pushed both of them away, "Whoa, ladies! Take it easy. I am not interested."

The blonde came closer to him, gently pulled his head and whispered in her ear, "Let us unite Britain, Japan and India tonight. Our place. I promise you'll see the stars."

Vivaan chuckled, then laughed. The girls looked at each other, puzzled. He gently took the blonde's hand and shook it. Then he did the same with the other girl. "Look! It was very nice meeting you both. You are Alisha, the rebel who hates her family. And you are Sakura, who needs to make ends meet," Vivaan said. Alisha was dumbstruck, as if the earth had moved from beneath her feet. Sakura felt fear on hearing her real name from a stranger.

Vivaan walked away.

"Wait! Wait!" Alisha stopped him. "How... how did you know our names?" she asked, flabbergasted.

"Listen, lady. I don't have a lot of time. If you can help me, I can help you out," Vivaan said.

Alisha looked at Sakura. Then Vivaan took them for dinner at the local restaurant. The ladies ordered beer and a ton of food. Vivaan was happy to treat them. Then, Sakura began to sob. "Hey! What's the matter?" Vivaan asked, pacifying her shoulder.

Alisha hugged her friend and looked at Vivaan. "She is just happy to be treated the right way. Nobody treats us well," she said.

"Then why are you in this profession?" Vivaan asked. "You have a college degree. Get a job and help Sakura too!" he said.

Alisha's jaw dropped again, and she gaped. "How...How could you possibly know that?" she asked, now a little scared too.

Then, Vivaan showed her and Sakura the translation on his cellphone. "That means, umm... shark... um... of," Alisha began piecing the language. Sakura froze in terror seeing the words on the screen. Vivaan saw her face go numb and cold. Alisha gently patted her shoulder and pulled her closer as she hushed her. Sakura was trembling a little.

"What happened? You know this person?" Asked Vivaan.

"Ohmih gosh! You are sweating, honey!" Alisha said, placing Sakura's head on her shoulder as she pacified her.

"Okay, don't say another word. Just let me hold your hand," Vivaan said, offering his hand. Sakura looked at Alisha with bunny eyes, then slowly let Vivaan hold her small, fragile hand. Vivaan sat straight in his chair, focusing on the medieval portrait of a knight that hung from the wall behind the two women. In the next second, he was in the realm of Sakura's past.

Little Sakura is hugging her Dakishimeru (抱きしめる), an indigo-coloured teddy bear. She is tucked in a warm blanket, her sleep interrupted by something. Through the roof, a sound comes in – someone has fallen on the floor. She recognizes the voice. Her mother screams. She can hear her groan. Sakura hears her mother's cries, begging for help.

She pushes her blanket away, holds her Dakishimeru close to her and walks out of the bedroom with bare feet. She hears her mother shriek in agony. Her little feet are struggling to climb the stairs, but they are not fast enough. As her mother's cries for help grow louder, she places her teddy bear on a step and trips on another. Her heart is racing. Little Sakura stands back and sees the bedroom door open. Through a 20 feet corridor, she reaches the bedroom door.

By now, her mother is no longer screaming. Little Sakura peeks through the half-open door. A tall, dark shadow blocks her sight. He is standing over a pair of bare legs. The body beneath the tall shadow is not moving. Something warm and moist touches her bare little feet. It is red and warm. She looks up. The tall dark figure is now looking at her. It slowly sits down to her eye level. It is a man. His face is sweating. He has no clothes on. The red, warm, moist thing is on his hands. Little Sakura is trembling. She wets herself. The man laughs. He holds her in his arms as he opens the door wide open. He begins strolling through the corridor, carrying little Sakura. As her eyes comprehend the truth, her mother's lifeless eyes say goodbye to her for the last time.

The man takes her downstairs. Sakura manages to grab her loved Dakishimeru from the stairs. The man notices this. He doesn't react to it. Sakura leaves the small cottage, her home near the marketplace, forever.

Vivaan's hand shivers as it leaves the woman's hand. His eyes are still fixed on the knight, slaying an outlaw on the ground. He looks into Sakura's glistening eyes. He comforts her by gently placing his warm hand on her cheek. "Do you know how this person... this shark, looks... or where he lives?" Vivaan asked.

Sakura wiped her tears and said as she sobbed, "I saw him only once. Many years ago." Alisha held her closer. Sakura continued, "He owns a nightclub nearby. But I guess nobody really sees him here. I have been dancing in his nightclub for years now."

Vivaan leaned forward, kept his hand over Sakura's, and asked, "Is he the man who killed your mom?"

The ladies' eyes went wide in horror. Alisha freaked out. "What you guys talkin' about?" She grabbed Sakura's hand, "Let's go. We want no nonsense from this guy. Thanks and no thanks for the dinner, mister," she said as she got up from the chair.

"Wanna try and hit on vulnerable women, jerk! Play this doofus psychic game with someone else. You'll get beaten, I am sure," Alisha went on a rant. But Sakura refused to join her. Instead, she kept looking at Vivaan, her jaw still dropped. She nodded in affirmation, looking into his eyes. Then a tear rolled down her plump white cheek. She smiled, burst into tears, of sorrow and hope as Vivaan fled the scene.

Alisha comforted and pacified her friend.

***

Vivaan walks out of the restaurant. He sets the destination to the Ichiban Nightclub (番ナイトクラブ). A few hundred meters into the main street, then to the left, right beside the steakhouse, he comes face to face with the Ichiban Nightclub. The large, well-lit display has tickers of alluring offers flashing over it. Booze, lap dances, private lounges, and a lot more. Vivaan scans the entrance to the premises. A black soundproof door and fire exit are guarded by two brawny Japs in the black. They have radios. A woman is standing behind the podium with an entry register.

Suddenly, a heavy downpour begins. Vivaan looks for shelter and instinctively runs towards Ichiban's entrance. The woman smiles at him, and he smiles back at her. Vivaan almost pushes the black entry door as one of the brawny chaps bars him with his hand. The lady walks over to him. But Vivaan is no longer present in the current situation. Through the slowly closing door, he gets to see a portrait in the lobby, whose walls are studded with red velvet. Vivaan automatically takes a step back, wrecked. The lady comes to him, smiles, and says in her Japanese accent - "Is you name on da list, Misuta?" Vivaan looks at her, shakes his head and turns back. He wished to take another look at what he had just seen. He knew what it was.

The rain becomes even more unforgiving and intense. He suddenly remembers the time when he's gone to Eiji's house party. He had seen the portrait of the same man there. Only, in this portrait, he stood with his two hounds from hell. The man in the portrait with his dogs was Hiroshi Minato - Eiji's Father, The Shark of Kabukicho, the robber behind Raptor M4's design... and now Vivaan's sworn enemy.

Lost in his thoughts, and knelt on the ground, Vivaan gets a call. Without seeing the screen, he picks the call, stifling under the burden of this newfound truth. Vivaan looks up to the sky as raindrops rinse his face.

Then, he hears Vidya's frantic voice - "Viv... Vivaan? Are you there? There's..." and she stutters and mumbles with fear. Her mother takes over the call. "Vivaan, Vivaan!" she says. Vivaan comes back to his senses in an instant, notices people by the sides of the street looking at him fallen on the ground. "Mom, what happened?" He asks, standing up and walking all drenched.

"I don't know what is happening, Vivaan! When are you coming back? *Beta...*" and her mother also breaks into tears. She continues speaking anyway. "Someone threw... someone threw a butchered animal in the compound last night. Dad and Vidya went out to see what happened. There were a few unidentified men... in...in a black car...and..."

"Mom! Mom... calm down, shhhh," Vivaan tried to infuse some peace in her. "Where is dad right now?" He asked.

"He went to file a police complaint," Amrita replied. "*Beta*, I don't know what is happening. Please be here soon," his mother cried.

"Don't worry mom, everything will be fine. I am sending Raunak back home. How is Shivani?" he asked.

"She...she is a little disturbed. But she is more worried about us," Amrita sobbed.

"Yeah...I know. Raunak will be at home ASAP. Have faith mom, I'll call you shortly. You stay brave, my *Mama*," Vivaan said restlessly, squeezing his hair. He immediately called Raunak as he motioned at a taxi for a ride.

"Hey, listen to me carefully," Vivaan said with all the calmness in his head. "I am in the cab. You need to go back to India. Our families are at risk, and you are the only one I trust right now," Vivaan said, getting inside a green electric vehicle.

"Hiroshi Minato, yeah... that same guy..." He continued to talk to puzzled Raunak. "He is a bad guy... a very bad guy... and now he is after me and my family."

"What?" Raunak asked.

"Yes. Raunak, listen to me. I'll tell you some truths that nobody knows. But right now, I want a favour from you. You handle the homeland turf; I'll sort things from here... Thanks! Thanks, buddy," Vivaan said as the silent electric cab raced towards the hotel.

Chapter 22

The clock struck 7pm, Tokyotime. The streets of Kabukicho came to life, untamed souls of the night began lurking. Singing birds climbed up into their cages to woo the lost souls, wolves scanned for the weak and vulnerable from the shabby corners of the dark lanes. The air felt untamed. Kabukicho wore its usual façade, and the night was soaked in colours of primal instincts driven by lust. The Ichiban nightclub was alive and a herd of lost souls found their way through an entry guarded by two beasts and handled by a singing bird.

Vivaan's cab stopped at the cross-section before the street's entrance, and he decided to walk to the club. His eyes no longer blinked for he had not slept the night before. They were sore and swollen, but Vivaan's sight was clear. He wore the frown of a king ready to launch an attack on the reign of terror. He walked out in all-black as if possessed by the determination of a killer. His gaze was fixated at the large display board of the Ichiban Club, and it grew larger as he got closer.

As he reached the entrance, he motioned at the lady with the guestlist to come over. The guards stood straight, reactionless, and alert. "May aa halpyounsaan?" She asked in a meek tone.

"I am on the guest list. Vivaan Shakya it is," Vivaan said, looking at his wristwatch. The lady scanned the list for names with a 'V' and soon got one. She smiled, almost apologetically, then motioned at one of the brawny guards to open the door. Vivaan went in and came face-to-face with a world that floated in an ether of mystery, obscenity, fear, and freedom.

There was a reception desk manned by an effeminate yet charismatic character. Two lobbies on either side of the desk opened into the club's main premises. Beside the left lobby lay a staircase that went up. Vivaan noticed the red band that made the staircase and the upper floor off-limits to the common folk. He then casually ignored the desk assistant and slowly walked to the right lobby. The bass of the gothic music grew louder. The red velvet walls absorbed some of it, but the treble went through one's ears, dissolving its senses. Vivaan stood before the portrait he had recognized the day before.

In the heavy gold-studded frame was affixed the image of Hiroshi Minato. Vivaan looked at it with a cold stare. The king's frown emerged on his face once again. He stopped a waitress, grabbed a whiskey on the rocks, and gestured at her to carry on. He then proceeded towards the treble and flashy lights of the lobby.

There, bodies of the lost souls melded with each other: some drunk enough to forget their pain, some drowned in the sweet agony of love. With every music beat and every other alcohol shot, the place invoked its inner animal that would come alive and devour all that was painful. Vivaan walked through the crowd of dancing, ruly and unruly men and women. He spotted a corner that seemed left out like the 2 ladies that sat there, engaged with their phones. He calmly covered one side of the black leather couch, and the ladies, dressed in shining, alluring clothes, sat opposite him. Vivaan gulped down the whiskey as it flowed passionately from between the ice rocks. He placed the glass on the table in front of him and began reading the room.

Then, he got up and went to the washroom across the lobby from where he sat. As he opened the door to the men's room, his shoulder with a bald Japanese guy, drunk to his breath. The Jap shoved Vivaan inside as he hurled unpleasant words at him. Vivaan regained his senses, smoothened his blazer and apologized to the man. The man put his hand inside the coat and casually pulled out a six-shooter. Vivaan froze. He slowly raised his hands - "It's all cool, brother!" he whispered. The inebriated man saw Vivaan in a servile position. He now pointed the revolver at him as he grinned. Vivaan felt his nerves go cold, but the whiskey inside his system bubbled in his blood. His heart pounded like a hammer and fists heated up like a cannonball.

As the man blinked to rub his eyes, Vivaan ducked and threw a punch at the man's face. A spurt of fresh blood flew out of his mouth and Vivaan grabbed the man's shooting hand. In the frenzy of the moment, as Vivaan struggled to grab the revolver, the man pulled the trigger. The 50 calibre S&W flashed and banged like a cannon. The lead shot went straight through the man's foot which he realized only after looking at it. The frenzy ended and Vivaan regained situational awareness. The men and women near the washroom lobby did not notice the shot amidst the drowning noise. Vivaan emptied the other 5 chambers of the revolver, dropped the gun in one of the stalls, and pulled the man inside the cubicle. A thick red mark followed what remained of his contorted foot. He howled like a savage in agony. Vivaan wiped the sweat off his face and quickly left the scene. As he exited the lobby, a bald Japanese bouncer with a thin moustache came face to face with him. Vivaan noticed him but ignored the guy. The bouncer did the same, but then he stopped, stared Vivaan for a few seconds with critical eyes and went inside the men's restroom.

Vivaan hurried towards the backdoor. He looked back twice, knowing that he was compromised. His cover was blown, and he needed to rush. Vivaan pushed the backdoor and entered a wide, rather quiet lobby. He pulled out his handkerchief and pretended to wipe his face as he walked around. There were numbered doors in the lobby. Vivaan put his ear against one of them. A waiter pushed a trolley of snacks and drinks and noticed Vivaan. He came closer, quietly. Vivaan drew his ear closer to the door. He could hear a few men and women clinking glasses.

"Saan?" The waiter called out to him. Vivaan was startled.

He turned around to see the trolley and the man behind it. Vivaan perspired, smiled nervously, and adjusted his blazer. Then, the emergency alarm went off. The premises blared with the sounds of caution. In a few seconds, the lobby became crowded. Some clothed and some nude, men and women came out of the rooms and looked at each other, trying to gauge the unknown threat around them. The waiter left the trolley and rushed into the disco lounge. The music was cutoff and a few women screamed. Vivaan knew the injured man had been discovered. Amidst the confusion and blaring sirens, he located a staircase at the end of the corridor.

Vivaan hung his sweat-stained blazer on a rack outside one of the doors and went down the stairs as people gathered around the stage area of the nightclub.

The stairs took him to the underground level where another narrow corridor spanned along the width of the building. At the end of the corridor, which was some 30 feet long, two metal cages were placed side-by-side. Behind those metal bars stood two alert, sharp and furious Rottweilers. They did not bark. Instead, they just looked at a frozen Vivaan who stared back at them.

Vivaan instinctively knew what or who they were protecting in the space behind them. He took one step forward; the dogs did not bark. He took another step towards them, they stood motionless, staring at him with bloodshot eyes. Their teeth shone like merciless blades of wrath and ferociousness. Slowly, Vivaan came face-to-face with the cages and the gate. The dogs growled continually in his presence, turning their heads at their prey who only breathed by the mercy of those metal bars.

Vivaan smiled. He placed his hand on the door and the dogs went berserk! They barked and chewed on the metal. Their drool could only be satisfied in the blood of the person that defied them and threatened their master's space. Then, Vivaan saw the key to the door, hanging from the collar of one of the hounds.

Vivaan ran back to the upper level to grab his blazer. He took it off the hanger and rushed to the dog cages, failing to notice a security guard who had just spotted him going off-limits.

Vivaan removed his shoes. Then, he wrapped the blazer tightly around his left hand to make a thick layer. He wore one shoe in the blazer-wrapped hand and neared it to the hound cage. The rottweiler growled and tried to grab the shoe. Then Vivaan took the whole hand behind bars. The dog pounded on it like freshly chopped meat. Vivaan felt the immense bone-crushing pressure but was saved from the bites. The dog pulled him inside the cage like a mad bull. Vivaan's face stuck close to the bars, but the dog's jaws remained clenched to his arm. He tried to grab the red, nail-studded dog collar with the other hand. The dog locked its jaw, and his blazer was tearing apart. Vivaan could now feel the canine's teeth reaching his flesh.

In a split second, before the dog could realize it, Vivaan pounced and grabbed the key with the other hand. The bone-crushing teeth now reached his flesh and Vivaan groaned. He was red with fear, exhausted and perspiring as his body struggled to pull the arm out. Vivaan slipped the shoe he wore in the hand. The hound did not budge. He then held the key in his mouth and dropped the other shoe in the cage to distract the dog. The hound grabbed the other shoe and Vivaan pulled his hand out.

Panting, terrified, and exhausted, he lay against the door, realizing both his newfound appreciation for life, and his newly discovered fear of big black dogs. Vivaan spat the key in his right hand. His left hand trembled and he knew it had a puncture wound from the bite. He tightened the blazer around it and began to unlock the door. In the light beneath his feet, he saw a shadow move at the far end of the corridor. Vivaan turned around and saw a man who looked at him. He was armed but the gun was in his holster. The man raised his hand, holding an unknown device.

Vivaan made no move. The man pressed the device which looked like a small remote. A distinct clicking sound erupted for a second. The dogs became alert, looking in the man's direction. Then Vivaan saw the cage doors fling open. His appreciation for life vanished again as his mouth formed the word - "S*it."

He hurried with the lock, his hands trembling. His heart was in his mouth. The dogs came out of the cages and turned around to catch the intruder. The handler dashed towards the door as Vivaan opened it and rushed in. The dogs headbutted into the door as Vivaan locked it from the inside.

***

It was a large hall with wooden and velvet walls. There were numerous artefacts placed immaculately around a heavy sandalwood table and a king's rocking chair. The top of the walls was lined with severed heads of every wild animal in the world's taxonomy. Vivaan immediately took out his cell phone and called Mahira. Even though the room's lead-plated roof allowed no signal to come or go through. Desperate for help, Vivaan switched on the location broadcast and SOS beacon on his phone for Mahira, Raunak and the Tokyo police. He held on to hope for good network coverage for them to find out his real situation.

Vivaan then straightway sat on the king's chair, facing the door, waiting to be apprehended. "Oh, God! Please let the police be the first ones to barge in here..." he mumbled to himself, sweating in fear. He put his left hand on the table and grabbed the armrest of the chair with the other. He then closed his eyes, still able to hear the footsteps clamouring outside the door.

Hiroshi is smoking in the room. There are only a few animal heads on the wall. Hiroshi Minato is furious. A man is kneeling before the table, his head bowed in submission, begging, and pleading Minato. 連れてって！ (Take him!) The man raises his head. He is an Indian man in a blue shirt, white trousers, and a tattered tie. His moustache is distinct, and his face resembles a forgotten memory. He is Jasmine's father, the man in the family portrait at Jasmine's ruined home. Two men with unclear faces come inside the room. They grab Kumar by his arms. He resists. Then Minato picks up a paper from the table. He hands it to one of the men and stands away, looking at a painting of Napoleon, puffing thick white smoke. One of the men takes Kumar's thumb, dips it in a pad of ink and forces it on the paper. The other pulls out a retractable baton and lashes Kumar in the back. He screams in pain, cries and shouts, "This is unfair! You can't do this to me... Please, I beg..." he goes on.

Minato turns back with a smug face. "I did it, Kumar," he speaks in a coarse yet calm voice. "Daisuke is mine!" his eyes shine like a wolf at night.

"No..." Kumar begs as the men drag him away.

"やめる！" Minato shouts. His men stop. "彼の娘も終わりなさい。 (Kare no musumemoowarinasai)," he utters. Kumar's eyes widened in terror. He becomes frantic, throwing his limbs around like an untamed mare. "No! No! Not my daughter! Spare her... Minato..." he shouts as the men drag him out of the room.

Vivaan comes out of the trance, his body frozen in time, his mind tipped out of reality. His ears become numb, even to the wild banging of the door which was about to be broken. Vivaan forgot to breathe for the next few moments. The thought of Jasmine's possible murder, all that he had known until now, Arpita, his family, his pain, his sense of love, Mahira, and everything his existence had encompassed till now flashed before his eyes.

The door finally broke. Vivaan sat there, lost in the ether of time. Five men barged in and grabbed a hold of Vivaan. One of them shoved his face on the table, the other held his hand against his back to restrain him. The bald guy from the restroom pulled his hair and spat in Vivaan's face. Vivaan was nearing the truth of ephemeral security in this fragile world. But another punch knocked him unconscious before he could even realize it.

Chapter 23

He coughed and spat, lying like a foetus alongside a moist wall. The room stank of stale air lost to the chaos of time. His eyes could see the restless dust particles dancing in the funnel of incoming light from the bulb hanging from the ceiling. Vivaan couldn't open his right eye. He gulped down saliva to wet his dry throat. A sharp jolt of pain ran through his jaw, and he groaned. He felt warm blood trickling from his nose. Then another shockwave of pain ran through his abdomen.

He pushed his body against the floor using his hands. Vivaan sat up and found himself in what appeared to be a cellar. It was poorly lit. There were a few old, rusted and leaking pipes running across the length of the back wall. The side walls were damp. Vivaan noticed a heavy jingling noise as he moved his feet. He saw a heavy flat-link chain cuffed around his ankle, the other end held by a cemented anchor. Vivaan gave a sharp jerk to the chain and kicked his leg in the air. The chain held it back with the strength of a thousand elephants.

He then searched his pockets. His cellphone was gone.

Hopeless and tired, Vivaan leaned against the wall and sat back on the floor.

"Hey!" He shouted at the top of this voice. "Hey…" Then Vivaan noticed a shadow approach the door through the gap below. It opened and the bald Japanese bouncer came to him, grabbed a handful of Vivaan's hair and smacked him in the face. Vivaan fell to the floor. Then another man came in. Vivaan saw his face. He was the bouncer who'd stood at the club's entrance. Vivaan resisted any other blow and shouted, "Hey! Stop…" but they didn't.

The second man splashed water on Vivaan's face. Vivaan panted and struggled to breathe. Then, he picked him up and held him against the right wall as the bald man cracked his knuckles. As soon as his face and chest touched the wall, he felt the incoming overload of visions and became nauseous.

The bald man straightened the baton and went open season on Vivaan's back. Vivaan felt nothing. The trance had taken him.

Jasmine is sitting on a chair placed in the middle of the room. Her hands are tied, and her mouth stuffed with a cloth. A young man, rather, a teenaged boy, enters the room. He is accompanied by a couple of men who stand just outside. The boy looks at Jasmine, who cries and pleads with him for mercy. The boy draws out a shiny, bloodthirsty sword. Jasmine's muffled screams grow louder in anticipation of what was to come.

Vivaan screams in horror at his vision. The baton reigns terror on its victim until the upper layer of his skin turns red and peels off. Vivaan, though, is too terrified to acknowledge the reality of his pain.

The young boy comes closer to Jasmine, his face revealing itself in the dull light above her. It is Eiji. Eiji places the tip of his sword on

Jasmine's chest, bows and holds the stance. Jasmine is exuding sweat. Her body trembles uncontrollably, and her muffled screams are no longer audible. Then, Eiji drives the sword right through her heart. Her lifeless legs kick in the air to relieve the unbearable agony of her dying body. Her hands almost tear through the thick rope she is bound with, as the blade emerges from the back of her shoulder blade. Then, silence prevails. Two men come with a shovel the next minute and Eiji orders them to dig out the right wall of the room. The third prepares concrete before Jasmine's lifeless body.

Now the pain stung Vivaan. It stung bad. The pain was fuming into a rage. The men became tired of working on their prisoner's body and wiped the sweat off their faces. They laughed at the sight of their lamb's blood-perfused body. Vivaan's bloodshot eyes faced the wall. For an unknown moment in the fabric of space-time, Jasmine's spectre emerged from the wall, kissed Vivaan and buried itself back into the wall. Vivaan grinned, then roared as he kicked back like a mad horse.

He grabbed the ear of one of the men and pulled him closer as his elbow choked him with formidable power. The bald guy threw two baton strikes on his arm. Vivaan didn't flinch. He then forced his elbow on the spine of the man he was holding. A loud 'snap' deterred the bald guy. He frantically looked for a safe space, but the door was several feet away. Vivaan already stood in front of him with the baton he had picked from the dead body. It was too late for the bald man. His last sight would probably have been Vivaan's eyes ridden by a primitive evil archetype of mother nature. The archetype that gave birth to the forms of warriors, vengeance, and justice. Vivaan broke the man's skull and soul with three lightning-fast baton strikes to his head.

The dripping water sounded like the music of victory in the background.

Vivaan then fell to the floor, lifeless.

***

Indistinct noises of men came through the door. Vivaan opened his eyes. He felt numb in the head. Suddenly, a burning sensation emerged in his back. Vivaan screamed and groaned in agony, much like a victim counting his final breaths in the burnward of a hospital. He saw the floor dust turn into mud as tears and mucus dripped from his eyes and nose. He coughed, trying to stand back up, but failed. Then he noticed a beam of a flashlight cut through the hole in the door. Vivaan cried like a newborn.

Someone kicked the door open, and multiple flashlights wreaked havoc inside the room. These men appeared to be coordinating with a lot of shouting. Vivaan turned his head to see what was happening but was blinded by the dazzling lights. He noticed multiple heavy, dark-coloured boots moving around him. Some pointed their lights at the fallen men around him. Then, one of them pointed at Vivaan's face with his light. By now, Vivaan had spotted residual smoke leaking inside the room. He tried to look outside the door. It was an unknown corridor, packed with dense smoke and a few bodies on the ground.

Then a man took out a cellphone and showed it to Vivaan. "Ijtheescerphaan your, san?" he asked. Vivaan looked at it and nodded a yes. 'SOS and location broadcast worked!' he thought to himself. Then the officer announced to his team as he shifted the focus of his rifle-mounted flashlight and the cell phone away from Vivaan's face, "ID正、司令官 (ID positive, commander." Fallen Vivaan briefly saw the 'SWAT' marking on one of the men's vests. Through the smoky corridor came in two men running with a stretcher. Vivaan knew he had been found. Then he felt his body being lifted by his shoulders and legs, with his face still down.

The men quickly took his pulse, checked for pupil dilation and rushed him out after putting on a mask on his face. Vivaan flew on the stretcher up the stairs. On the upper deck, he saw that he was still in the Ichiban nightclub. The club had become a ghost town. There were a few bodies lying here and there, all shot with precision.

As the men exited the premises, Vivaan grabbed a police officer's hand, causing the men to stop abruptly. He asked the police officer to come near to him, and he did. "San, how maa aye help?" the officer asked. Vivaan was too weak to speak lucidly. He just uttered a few words, "Torture room, right wall... dig... the right wall." The officer quickly noted his unclear words in a small notepad, and the men rushed Vivaan into an ambulance.

The scene outside the Ichiban club was laced with throngs of people. Kabukicho street hadn't witnessed a SWAT operation for more than a decade. News helicopters swarmed the street with LIVE aerial coverage of the shootout's aftermath. Every radio within the 1-kilometre radius was crackling. The *Shark of Kabukicho* has been exposed.

***

5 Days later

Vivaan wakes up in a cosy bed, to the voice of television to his left. To his right, a windowpane welcomes sunshine with open arms. He notices special cushioning and support under his back. He turns his head to the left and sees a familiar figure watching television.

"Raunak?" Vivaan mumbles. Raunak, surprised, mutes the TV and turns to Vivaan. "Hey, buddy! Thought you were gonna sleep longer today as well!" Raunak said with a grand smile.

"Today? How... how long have I..." Vivaan asked, his lips twitching to the residual pain.

"Shh...don't say anything. Just see," Raunak said as he changed the channel and unmuted the TV.

A blonde news reporter on UK Channel 4 reported a piece of breaking news. *'After the police crackdown at the Ichiban nightclub in Tokyo city, an older dead body has been recovered from one of the underground storage chambers. The body had been cemented inside a wall, and is allegedly of Jasmine Kumar, the woman automotive pioneer from India, who disappeared years ago.'*

Vivaan sat up, his eyes tried to comprehend the truth. The TV reporter continues, *'Following the crackdown, Harisho Minato and his son Eiji Tanaka committed suicide two days ago. The investigators are looking for any other loose ends in the case.'*

Raunak looks at Vivaan. "I have another surprise for you," he says. Then, Mahira enters the room and sits by Vivaan's side on the bed. Raunak makes an excuse and exits the room. Vivaan is dumbstruck by her presence, overwhelmed, and thankful. She nudges him to not utter a word. Vivaan's eyes glisten with tears. Mahira strokes his hair then kisses him on the forehead. With tearful eyes, he enunciates 'Thank you' with his lips for saving his life.

"Let's go home. I have your mom's permission," Mahira says with a smile as she takes him in her arms.

***

An open Suzuki Samurai jeep stops before Jasmine's old house. Vivaan looks at her room's window. "This is the house you were telling me about?" Mahira asks. Vivaan keeps looking at the windowpane, nodding to Mahira's question.

Then, almost like a vision, Jasmine appears through the window of her old room. She looks at Vivaan with graceful eyes. Her smile is eternal as always. She is wearing the orange gown she wore at the time of her demise. She blows a flying kiss towards Vivaan. His heart becomes light, and his soul unburdens. A tear rolls down his eye. He looks at Mahira, embraces her and kisses her. Then he looks back at the windowpane. Jasmine is gone.